Chapter 1

I was all alone in my back garden.

Except, that is, for the spaceship that had landed there just a few seconds earlier.

If I'd had any sense, I'd have turned around and bolted. Instead, though, I stood there, transfixed by the grey and silver vessel that had just squashed my favourite lupins. Suddenly, there was a hissing sound, and a small round hatch on top of the spaceship began to open slowly.

Moments later, one of the strangest creatures I'd ever seen emerged. And, trust me, I've seen a few strange creatures in my time. Mr Hosey for starters.

I wasn't sure if the creature was wearing an armoured suit or if the metal was in fact its body. It had two arms, two legs and a head, but no face as far as I could make out. What it lacked in height (it was no more than three feet tall), it made up for in physique. This guy was buff; it must have had a membership at Gym Alien.

Wherever it had come from, it hadn't travelled here alone because within a matter of seconds, a dozen identical creatures joined it on the wings of the ship.

"Hi, guys." I gave them a friendly wave and treated them to my 'Welcome to planet Earth' smile.

No response. How rude.

Maybe they didn't speak the language, but would it have killed them to return my wave?

Oh wait! Perhaps I'd been a little too quick to judge because the head alien began to raise its arm. It soon became apparent that it wasn't about to wave. Instead it pointed its arm at me as though it was lining me up in its sights.

Cripes! I only just managed to dodge whatever kind of weird alien bullet it had fired. And now the others were taking aim at me too. This was it. I was doomed.

"Jill, wake up." Someone nudged me.

I sat up with a start and was filled with a great sense of relief as I realised it had only been a dream.

"I was having a nightmare."

"I could tell." Jack grinned. "You were shouting *don't shoot.*"

"A spaceship had landed in our back garden, and these horrible metal creatures got out. They were trying to kill me."

"It must be the aftereffects of the wind turbines incident. The Udders, or whatever they were called."

"Oodahs. Yeah, I reckon you're right." I jumped out of bed and hurried onto the landing.

"What are you doing now?" Jack called after me.

"Just checking the back garden."

"It was only a nightmare, Jill."

"Better safe than sorry."

Twenty minutes later, we were in the kitchen, eating breakfast.

"I wish I could see that waxwork of you," Jack said.

"Unless you can figure out a way to go to Candlefield, that's never going to happen."

"You could take a photograph, couldn't you?"

"That depends how bad it is."

"When is it going to be ready, anyway?"

"They said it would probably take a couple of weeks. I assume somebody will give me a call when it's finished."

Just then, there was a knock at the door; it was our next-door neighbour, Britt.

"Morning, you two. I'm sorry to call around so early."

"That's okay," Jack said. "We were just discussing Jill's waxwork."

It was usually me who spoke before I'd engaged my brain, but this time Jack had surpassed himself.

"Waxwork?" Unsurprisingly, Britt looked more than a little taken aback by this revelation.

Panic-stricken, Jack turned to me for help in getting himself out of the hole he'd just dug.

"No." I laughed. "Not *waxwork*. We were discussing my — err — *tax work*. I hate tax returns, don't you?"

"Err, yeah." By now, Britt was thoroughly confused, but thankfully, she let it drop and moved onto the subject she'd come around to discuss. "Kit and I are running the Washbridge marathon this Saturday."

That was my cue to get in quickly before Jack had the chance to volunteer us for something that I'd regret. "I'm sorry Britt, but we won't be able to take part. We're already committed to doing something on Saturday. It's a pity, but what can you do?"

She smiled. "That's not why I'm here. And anyway, it's too late to sign up for the marathon now. The applications closed several weeks ago."

Phew!

"The reason I called around was to ask if you'd like to sponsor Kit and me."

"We'd love to," Jack said, and then winced, as I kicked him on the ankle.

"That's very kind." She handed him the clipboard.

"How does it work?" Jack was way too keen to give away our cash.

"They're doing things a little differently this year. Solo runners still get sponsorship in the usual way, but couples get paid for their combined results. So, for example, if you sponsor Kit and me, you pay for the combined mileage that we cover."

"Isn't that exactly the same thing?" I said.

"Kind of, but there's also the duo bonus." She pointed to the form. "That little check box there."

"What's that for?" Jack asked.

"If both of us were to break the three-hour mark, the amount you pay is increased slightly."

"Okay." Jack picked up the pen. "How much shall I put, Jill?"

"How about a penny a mile?"

"Jill is such a joker." He shot me a look. "How about fifty pence a mile?"

"Fifty-pence?" I almost choked. "I assume you both expect to finish?"

"Oh yes," she said, confidently. "We've been training for months."

"So, that's twenty-six miles times two, isn't it? I make that fifty-two miles."

"Fifty-pence sounds just about right, then." Jack had filled in the form before I had chance to stop him.

"That's very generous." Britt snatched back the clipboard, presumably before I could grab it and reduce the amount. "Thank you so much. Both of you."

After Britt had left, Jack said, "Why are you looking at me like that?"

"Fifty-pence per mile? What were you thinking? What was wrong with ten-pence?"

"Don't be so tight. They're our neighbours. And, anyway, it's for a good cause."

Before I could point out the error of his ways, my phone rang; it was Kathy.

"If you want me to sponsor you for something, the answer is no," I snapped.

"What are you talking about, Jill?"

"Nothing, it doesn't matter. Jack's just doing his best to bankrupt us."

"I only rang to ask when I can meet Martin."

"How would I know?"

"Come on, Jill, I want to meet the guy. What's he like, anyway?"

"Okay, I guess."

"*Okay*? Is that it?"

"He and Jack get on like a house on fire. They've already been bowling together, and they're both into model trains. Jack has seen way more of him than I have."

"So, when can I see this new brother of yours?"

"I'll speak to him and ask when he's available."

"I know you, Jill. As soon as you put the phone down, you'll forget about it."

"I won't. I promise. I'll contact him today. Tomorrow at the latest."

"And you'll let me know?"

"Yes, yes, I'll let you know, but I have to get going now."

"Okay. Catch you later."

"That was Kathy, I assume?" Jack said.

"Yeah. She wants to meet Golden Boy."

"I assume you mean Martin."

"Who else?"

"I don't know why you've got it in for him. He's a great bloke."

"Maybe, but there's something about him that I don't trust."

"Your problem, Jill, is that you don't trust anyone."

"Given some of the characters I come across in my work, that's hardly surprising."

"What are you working on at the moment?"

"Nothing much. I'm between cases. What about you? Anything interesting happening in West Chipping?"

"I'm working on a case involving a man who disappeared from a hotel."

"Disappeared as in —?"

"As in vanished into thin air."

***

When I left the house, there was a zebra and a pelican on next-door's front garden.

My neighbours, Tony and Clare, were obsessed with cosplay, and these were no doubt their latest costumes.

"Hey, you two. I like those."

"Thanks, Jill," said the pelican, AKA Clare. "It's certainly an improvement on the boomerang."

"Can you guess what con we're going to this week, Jill?" said the zebra, AKA Tony.

"Is it ZooCon?"

"Not even close." Claire laughed.

"I don't have a clue. You're going to have to tell me."

"It's RoadSafetyCon," Tony said.

"*Road Safety*? Sorry, you've lost me."

"I'm a zebra crossing, and Clare is a pelican crossing.

Get it?" They both laughed. Clearly, they were easily amused.

The best I could muster was a smile. "Good luck at the con."

When I arrived at the toll bridge, Mr Ivers looked very sad.

Yes, I know he's the epitome of *sad*, but today he looked particularly downcast. And, significantly, there wasn't a hand puppet to be seen.

"Morning, Mr Ivers. Why no hand puppets today?"

"I'm not really in the mood for them, Jill, to be honest."

"What's the matter? Aren't you feeling well?"

"My heart has been broken. Ivy has found herself another beau."

I assumed that was his way of saying he'd been dumped.

"Oh dear. I'm very sorry to hear that."

"She's gone off with another puppeteer and his marionettes."

"Marion who?"

"Not Marion. *Marionettes*. You know — string puppets. I feel so betrayed."

"These things happen, I'm afraid. Still, there are plenty more fish in the sea."

"I'm beginning to think I might have run out of bait, Jill. It's a pity that you are already spoken for. I've always thought that we'd make a great couple."

Not from where I was standing.

"Anyway, I must get going." I handed him the cash. "Places to meet. People to go. And all that. Try to keep your chin up. There's someone out there for you somewhere, I'm sure."

Even though the guy drove me insane, I couldn't help but feel rather sorry for Mr Ivers. He and Ivy had seemed like the perfect couple.

***

When I arrived at the office, Mrs V looked exhausted: Her eyes were heavy, she was yawning, and she looked as though she might fall asleep at any moment.

"Are you okay Mrs V? Are you coming down with something?"

"No dear." She yawned. "It's not that." She glanced around the room, as though she thought someone might be eavesdropping, then she said in a whisper, "It's Armi, dear. He's—err— I'm not sure I should tell you this."

"Go on. You know you can tell me anything."

"The thing is, Jill, just lately he's been rather more frisky than usual."

"Oh?" That was the last thing I'd expected her to say.

"I don't know where he's getting all that energy from. Take last night for instance, he—"

I was all for sharing, but this was way too much information.

"Was that my phone?"

"I didn't hear anything."

"Yes, I'm sure it was. I'll catch up with you later, Mrs V."

"All right, dear."

As soon as I walked into my office, the first thing I noticed was the gold trophy standing on my desk.

Winky, who was seated on the sofa, shuddered. "I feel unclean."

"What are you talking about?"

"What do you think I'm talking about? The old bag lady of course. All that talk about her and her old geezer getting frisky. It's enough to turn your stomach. It shouldn't be allowed at her age."

"Don't be ridiculous. It's perfectly healthy."

"How come you did a runner when she tried to give you all the gory details, then?"

"I didn't. I thought I heard my phone."

"Of course you did. Anyway, enough of that. Haven't you noticed anything?" He gestured towards my desk.

"Yes, the desk is looking so much better since you removed the decoupage."

"Not that. I'm talking about what's standing on it."

I looked again. "Oh, you mean the trophy. I hadn't noticed that. Is it yours?"

"It most certainly is. You are looking at the Best Dressed Cat in Washbridge."

"Don't tell me you won."

"Of course I won. It was never in any doubt. I'm now through to the national competition. When I win that, I'll pick up a cool five grand."

"*When*? Aren't you rather counting your chickens?"

"Not at all. It's a foregone conclusion. And it's not just the prize money. There's all the endorsement opportunities that will follow."

Thankfully, by the time Mrs V brought through my mid-morning cup of tea, she seemed to have forgotten about Armi's newfound friskiness.

"Incidentally, Mrs V, there's something I've been meaning to tell you."

"Yes, dear?"

"Well, the thing is — err — this is going to sound kind of weird."

"I'm used to that from you, dear. What is it?"

"It turns out that I have a brother."

"Oh? I see." She pondered on it for a few moments. "Actually, no, I don't see at all. What do you mean you have a brother?"

"It's very complicated. You know I was adopted?"

"Of course, dear."

"Well it appears my birth mother had a child before me; a little boy."

"Why have you never mentioned him before?"

"Because I didn't know he existed. Like I said, it's complicated."

"You must be excited."

"Err, yes. Very."

"Well that is a surprise. I'm very pleased for you."

"Thanks."

"I was going to ask if you and Jack would like to come over for dinner some time? We'd love to see you both, and it'll give you the chance to have a proper look around the house."

"Err, sure, but I'll need to check with Jack to see what days he can do. Is it okay if I get back to you?"

"Of course, dear."

"I should steer well clear of that if I were you," Winky said, after Mrs V had left the room.

"What are you talking about?"

"You heard what the bag lady said about her and Frisky Armi. Goodness knows what she has planned when you and Jack go around there."

"Don't be so disgusting."

"Don't say I didn't warn you. And what's all this codswallop about a long-lost brother?"

"You heard what I told Mrs V."

"Yes, I did, but unlike the old bag lady, I'm not a gullible idiot."

"What have I told you about being rude about Mrs V?"

"Come on. What's the real story?"

"Okay, if you must know, he's been living in another version of Candlefield."

"Isn't that the weird paranormal place you disappear to all the time?"

"That's right."

"And this brother of yours lives in a parallel version of Candlefield."

"That's it exactly."

"Oh boy. I wouldn't want to be inside your brain. What's he like, then? This brother of yours?"

"I barely know him yet. He looks like me."

"Poor guy."

"And he seems smart like me."

"He can either be smart. Or he can be like you. He can't be both, so which is it?"

Before I could lay into Winky, Harold, the pigeon, appeared on the window ledge.

"Morning, Jill." He waved a wing. "Morning, Winky."

"Hey, Harold." Winky jumped onto my desk. "What do you think of my trophy?"

"It's fabulous. What did you win it for?"

"Guess."

"Entrepreneur of the year?"

"Close. You're looking at Washbridge's best dressed cat."

"Well done." He turned to me. "Jill, I hate to ask, but I need a favour."

"What can I do for you?"

"Ida's sister wants to pay us a visit."

"That'll be nice for them both."

"It will if she can find her way here. Emma has never been here before, and her homing instinct never was very good, but recently it's deteriorated to the point where she can't find her way from point A to point B without assistance."

"Oh dear. How can I help?"

"Would you download an app called Pigeon Router? You should find it in the app store."

"Let me take a look." I took out my phone. "Yes, it's here."

"Would you mind installing it?"

"Okay." It took only a few seconds. "Right. What now?"

"Do you see a button marked 'I'm Here'?"

"Yeah."

"Press that."

"Okay. Now it's asking for a name."

"Type 'Harold' and then press 'Go'."

"H-A-R-O-L-D. Okay. I've pressed 'Go'. What now?"

"That's all. That will send out a signal for Emma to follow. She should be here within the hour. Thanks, Jill."

"No problem."

Chapter 2

The morning was really dragging.

I was in-between cases, and I had very little to occupy my mind. I'd spent the last hour doing one of my least favourite jobs: Preparing for the visit of my accountant, Luther Stone. Bookkeeping had always been something of a mystery to me; a necessary evil that got in the way of my real work. Why anyone would choose to be an accountant, I couldn't begin to imagine. I'd rather poke my eyes out with a red-hot poker.

By ten-thirty, I was practically comatose from boredom, when Mrs V came through to my office.

"There's a woman out there, Jill. She called in on spec and wondered if you might spare her a few minutes."

"I'd be happy to. Anything to get away from this paperwork. What's her name?"

"Mrs Cross."

"Okay, show her in, would you?"

In her early forties, Mrs Cross was well dressed without being showy. She clearly had an eye for fashion, much like me.

"Thank you for seeing me without an appointment, Mrs Maxwell." She offered me a confident hand. "I'm sure you're very busy."

"Call me Jill, please. I'm actually extremely busy at the moment, but I do have a few minutes to spare before my next meeting."

Over on the sofa, Winky was grinning at me, but I ignored him.

"Do have a seat, Mrs Cross."

"You must call me Lorraine."

"How exactly can I help you today, Lorraine?"

"I'm here about my brother, Eddie Broom. He went missing from a hotel."

That rang a bell. Earlier that morning, Jack had told me that he was working on a case that involved a man who had vanished from a hotel in West Chipping.

"Actually, Lorraine, I think I heard something about that. I'm not usually in the business of turning clients away, but I do think it might be best to give the police a little time to investigate before you hire a private investigator."

"They've already had two years. How much longer should I give them?"

"Sorry, I must have misunderstood. I was talking about a man who went missing under similar circumstances within the last few days. From a hotel in West Chipping."

"Actually, it was seeing that story in the newspaper today that prompted me to take matters into my own hands. The police have had more than enough time to find out what happened to Eddie, so it's up to me now."

"I see. Perhaps it would be best if you started by telling me exactly what happened two years ago?"

"Eddie was visiting Washbridge for a few days on business, and was staying at the Parkside Hotel. Do you know it?"

"I do, yes. Is there any reason he didn't stay with you?"

"I don't actually live in Washbridge. I live in a village called Middle Tweaking. You probably haven't heard of it. Not many people have."

"As it happens, I was there only a few weeks ago. Do you know Myrtle Turtle?"

"Everyone knows Myrtle."

"She's a friend of mine. Anyway, you were saying your brother had booked into the Parkside?"

"Yes, for three days, but according to the hotel staff, no one saw him after the first day. His bed had never been slept in."

"Was it the hotel who reported his disappearance?"

"No, it was his wife, Sandra." Lorraine hesitated. "Eventually."

"*Eventually?*"

"It wasn't until two days after he should have returned home that she thought to contact the police."

"Why the delay?"

"She maintains that she wasn't worried because he often returned late from business trips."

"Did he pay you a visit while he was up here?"

"No. I didn't even know he was in the area."

"What line of business was your brother in?"

"He worked for a company called Branded Context. They're an advertising agency. He never told me much about his work."

"Were you close?"

"Not as close as we used to be before he married that cow."

"I take it you and she don't get along?"

"He should never have married that awful woman. I never liked her. After he disappeared, I was frantic. I kept calling the police to ask what they were doing. I think they got fed up with me in the end. Not Sandra though. She didn't seem to care that her husband had disappeared."

"People do react in different ways when this kind of thing happens. Maybe she's just good at hiding her feelings."

"If she was so upset, how come she found herself a new man less than six months after Eddie disappeared?"

Lorraine Cross proceeded to tell me everything she knew about her brother's disappearance, which in all honesty, didn't amount to much at all. If she was to be believed, the police clearly thought her brother had deliberately gone missing, and subsequently they'd put only the minimum resources into the case.

"Okay, Lorraine, I think I have everything I need for now. I'll be in touch if I think of anything else."

"Thank you for taking this on. You're my last hope."

No pressure, then.

"Extremely busy?" Winky scoffed. "You were just sitting there, twiddling your thumbs until she walked through the door."

"I don't remember asking for your input."

"What you need is an innovative marketing campaign."

"Let me guess. You just happen to be an expert marketeer."

"As it happens, I am. And for you, I'm prepared to put together a campaign that is bound to bring in new clients. And what's more, I'd be willing to do it for a vastly reduced fee."

"I'm not interested."

"You haven't heard how much it would cost yet."

"Would it be free?"

"Of course not."

"Then I'm not interested."

"Are you sure? This is a once in a lifetime offer. Never to be repeated."

"Watch my lips. I. Am. Not. Interested."

***

My phone rang; it was Martin.

"You don't mind me calling you again, do you, Sis?"

Until recently, I'd had no idea that I had a brother, so you might think that I'd want to see him at every opportunity, but, to be perfectly honest, I still didn't completely trust the man, even though I didn't know why.

"Of course not, Martin. I love to hear your voice. Actually, I was speaking to Kathy earlier this morning. She wanted to know when she could see you."

"I can't wait to meet her, but I'm actually tied up every evening this week. I can more or less do any night next week. Do you think we could arrange something for then?"

"Why don't I have a word with her, to see which days she's free, and I'll let you know?"

"That works for me."

"Great. Now, what was it you called me for?"

"Nothing, really. I just fancied a quick chat."

"Right. Well, it's been great talking to you, but I'll have to go now because my next client is due at any minute."

"We should have a lie jar in here," Winky said. "If you put fifty pence in it every time you lied, it would be full within a month."

"Don't exaggerate. I hardly ever tell a lie."

"That's the first fifty-pence, right there."

I needed to check with Kathy which days she was free

the following week, but rather than phone her, I decided to kill two birds with one stone. I was gagging for a drink, and I figured if I nipped down to Kathy's shop, I could get a free cup of coffee and some biscuits.

"I'm going to Kathy's for a while, Mrs V. I shouldn't be very long."

"All right, dear. While you were talking to Mrs Cross, you had a phone call from Luther Stone, to confirm he'll be coming in tomorrow. He wanted me to remind you to make sure you had everything prepared for him."

"That's okay. It's all in hand."

When I arrived at Kathy's Bridal Shop, she was busy with some customers. One of them, clearly the bride-to-be, was trying on a dress. Kathy was on her hands and knees, pinning it up, under the watchful eye of an older woman who was obviously the bride's mother.

Kathy spotted me. "Jill, I'm on my own in here today. Would you be a darling and go into the back, and bring through those two cerise bridesmaids' dresses?"

I looked at her blankly. "Cerise?"

"Yes, please."

"Right."

In the back there were two racks of bridal gowns, and several more racks of bridesmaids' dresses, but which were the 'cerise' ones? What colour was cerise? I had no idea, but I seemed to recall it was a shade of red, so I picked out the first red ones on the rack and took them through to the shop.

Both the bride and her mother looked horrified.

"I said the cerise ones," Kathy snapped. "Those are maroon."

"I thought cerise was red."

"Cerise is a vivid reddish pink. Go and have another look."

What was it with all these stupid colour names? Why couldn't people just call them what they were? If she'd said, *get me the vivid reddish pink bridesmaids' dresses*, I might have had a chance of getting it right the first time.

I put the maroon dresses back on the rail and picked up the cerise (shouldn't be a real word) ones.

"Thanks." Kathy took them from me. "Have a seat. I shouldn't be much longer."

Fifteen minutes later, when the bride and her mother finally left the shop, I was sure I heard her say something that sounded a lot like *colour blind*.

"Are all your customers as difficult as those two?"

"They weren't difficult. You should see some of the clients I get in here."

"Any chance of a cuppa?"

She gave me a look. "You could have made one while you were waiting."

"It tastes better when you make it."

"Is that the only reason you popped in? For a free drink?"

"Actually, I came to tell you that I've spoken to Martin."

"Did you ask when I could meet him?"

"I did."

"What did he say?"

"Make me a cuppa, and I'll tell you."

Grumbling under her breath, she went into the back and made us both a coffee.

"Ginger nuts?" I screwed up my face. "Is that all you've

got?"

"Take them or leave them. Now, what did Martin have to say?"

"He's busy all this week, but he said that he's free everyday next week."

"I've just had a great idea."

Never a good thing. "What's that?"

"Why don't we 'siblings' get together? Just the three of us? Pete and Jack can go bowling."

"That's fine by me."

"How about next Tuesday? A week tomorrow?"

"Okay. I'll let Martin know. Where do you want to do it? At your house?"

"Yeah. I'll try and get Pete's parents to have the kids."

As I made my way back up the high street, Betty Longbottom stepped out of The Sea's The Limit.

I had to do a doubletake because she looked so different from the last time I'd seen her. She had a new hairstyle, was wearing way more makeup than usual, and had obviously splashed out on a new navy-blue suit.

"Good morning, Mrs Maxwell." For some reason, she was putting on a weird posh accent. And why on earth was she calling me Mrs Maxwell?

"Good morning, Betty."

"Mrs Maxwell, I just wanted to thank you for the positive review of The Sea's The Limit that you submitted to The Bugle."

This was getting weirder and weirder. First, she calls me Mrs Maxwell—something she'd never done before. And now she thanks me for a review I knew nothing about. I had never left a review, positive or otherwise, in

The Bugle.

Before I could correct her, she continued, "Yes, that's true, Mrs Maxwell. There has indeed been a one hundred percent increase in attendances in the last few months."

It was only then that I spotted them: Inside the shop, were a film crew who were recording this exchange through the open door. Everything made sense now. They were filming the reality TV show; the one I'd been offered, but which I'd declined. Betty was clearly trying to put on a good spin for the benefit of the TV audience.

I figured that I owed it to her to play along, so I said, "In my opinion, The Sea's The Limit is the best entertainment venue in all of Washbridge. You are to be commended on what you have done here."

"That's very kind of —" She stopped mid-sentence, and her expression turned from one of gratitude to one of shock. "You've got a pigeon on your shoulder, Jill." Gone now, was the posh voice.

But she wasn't wrong because perched on my left shoulder, there was indeed a pigeon.

"So I do. Where did that come from?"

This clearly wasn't the kind of image that Betty was hoping to project, so she made her excuses and scurried back inside the shop.

Meanwhile, the pigeon was staring at me. "Where's Ida?"

That's when the penny dropped. I'd totally forgotten about the pigeon app.

"Are you Ida's sister?"

"Yes, I'm Emma. Who are you?"

"My name's Jill. I'm a friend of Ida's. Harold asked me to set up the app to send you directions to get here."

"I don't understand." She glanced around. "Where are Ida and Harold?"

"I'm very sorry. I had to nip out of the office, and I'd totally forgotten that you were headed over here. Harold and Ida are just up the road. I can point the way if you like."

"I wouldn't trust myself to find them," she said. "My sense of direction is terrible. Do you think you could take me there?"

"I suppose so."

So it was that I continued up the high street with a pigeon on my left shoulder. Needless to say, I attracted a few strange looks along the way.

How would I explain this to Mrs V? She would think I'd finally lost the plot. Somehow, I had to get her out of the office for a few minutes, so I could take Emma through to the window ledge.

I took out my phone and made a call. My plan was to send her on an errand to the shop. The phone rang out, but there was no reply; she must have nipped to the loo. This was my chance.

I hurried up the stairs, through the outer office, into my office and over to the window where I placed Emma gently onto the ledge.

"Ida and Harold are just down there on the left."

"Thanks, Jill."

When I turned around, Mrs V was standing in the doorway, giving me the strangest look. "Who are Ida and Harold? And why were you talking to a pigeon?"

Chapter 3

"See what I mean?" Winky laughed. "That jar would already be half full."

"What are you talking about now?"

"The lie jar I suggested we should have in here. You've just spent the last five minutes lying to the old bag lady about what happened with the pigeons."

"Those were extenuating circumstances. I had to think on my feet."

"It's a good thing she's so gullible. Who else would have believed that you just happened to come across a racing pigeon that your neighbour had lost?"

I took out my phone. "How am I supposed to switch this stupid pigeon app thingy off?"

"You're hopeless." Winky held out his paw. "Give it here."

"Are you sure you know what you're doing?"

"Course I do. It's simple." He twiddled around for a few seconds and then handed the phone back to me. "There, all done. Simples."

Lorraine Cross had painted a somewhat damning picture of her brother's wife, Sandra, but I wanted to make my own assessment of the woman, to see if she was as bad as Lorraine had portrayed her to be.

"Is that Sandra Broom?"

"Speaking."

"My name is Jill Maxwell. I wonder if I could speak to you about your husband, Eddie."

"His name was Edward. And who exactly might you be, Ms Maxwell?"

"I'm a private investigator."

"Why are you interested in Edward? Who hired you?"

"Your husband's sister."

"Lorraine? I might have known. She had no right to do that."

"She's only interested in discovering what—"

"I have nothing to say to you. Goodbye."

"But Mrs—" It was too late—she'd already hung up.

If that brief exchange was anything to go by, it seemed that Lorraine Cross was right about Sandra Broom. What a nasty piece of work. Still, I was nothing if not persistent, so I tried again.

"Mrs Broom?"

"You again? I've already told you that—"

"If you could just spare me a few minutes of your time. That's all it would take."

"Don't call me again or you'll have my lawyer to deal with. Goodbye."

Clearly, I was going to get nowhere with that woman. One thing that she'd said did strike me as curious. She said his name *was* Edward. Past tense. Was that significant? Did she know something I didn't?

***

Barry had been a little under the weather over the weekend, so I magicked myself over to Aunt Lucy's, to check on how he was doing.

As soon as I walked through the door, I could hear raised voices coming from the kitchen; Aunt Lucy and Lester were arguing. I was just about to turn around and leave when she spotted me through the open door.

"Don't just stand there, Jill. Come on in."

"Are you sure? If this is a bad time, I can—"

"Don't be silly. Come on in."

"I was just about to leave, anyway." Lester stood up. "When Lucy's in this kind of mood, there's no point in trying to reason with her." With that, he stormed out of the kitchen and out of the house.

Aunt Lucy raised her eyebrows. "Men!"

"I'm sorry if I called at an inconvenient time."

"That husband of mine is driving me insane. Do you know what he's done this time?"

"It's really none of my business."

"He's applied for another job."

"I thought you'd be pleased about that. You hate him working as a grim reaper."

"That's true, but the new job is even worse."

"Worse than a grim reaper? What could possibly be worse than that?"

"The fool has only gone and applied to train as a dragon slayer."

"I didn't know such things existed."

"To be perfectly honest, neither did I until he told me what he'd done. Apparently, the city authorities employ a few of them; they work just beyond the dark woods. Their job is to make sure none of the dragons venture into the suburban area of Candlefield."

"Surely that must be dangerous."

"Dangerous is an understatement. From the little research I've managed to do on the subject, it appears there's a fatality rate of almost twenty-five per cent in that line of work."

"You can't let Lester do that."

"That's what I've been trying to tell him ever since I found out what he was planning, but he has his heart set on it now."

"Why, though? What's the appeal?"

"The money mainly. As you'd expect, they have to pay extremely high salaries. How else would they get anyone to do it?"

"Would you like me to have a word with him?"

"It wouldn't do any good, Jill. The man is too obstinate. Anyway, let's talk about something else. All this dragon-slayer stuff is giving me a headache. I'll put the kettle on."

Once we had our drinks, we went through to the lounge.

"How did your sitting at the waxworks go?"

"It wasn't quite the ordeal I'd expected, but the man who did it was horrible. He barely said a word to me all the time I was there. I was told afterwards that he doesn't approve of celebrities or sports stars being granted wax models. He thinks it should be restricted to artists."

"Such snobbery. Do you know when it'll be ready?"

"In a couple of weeks, I think."

"You must let us know when it's on display. We all want to see it; the twins have talked about nothing else."

"How are the twins?"

"They're fine. They came over here for Sunday lunch yesterday."

"Do they ever invite you to *their* houses for Sunday lunch?"

"That's a joke, I assume." She laughed. "I'm not sure either one of them has ever made a Sunday lunch. It doesn't matter because I love having them all over here. It's just a pity Jack is a human. It would be nice if you and he could join us too."

"Maybe I should trade him in and marry a sup instead."

Aunt Lucy looked horrified.

"I'm only joking. I wouldn't swap Jack for anyone." I hesitated. "Unless, of course, they were filthy rich."

"Jill!"

"Still joking. How are those new neighbours of yours?"

"To tell you the truth, I haven't seen much of them. From what they said, the baby should arrive any day now. They're probably busy preparing for that."

***

I needed bread and milk, so I called in at The Corner Shop on my way home. As usual, Little Jack was on stilts behind the counter. Curiously, he was dressed only in shorts and a vest top, and he looked very flustered indeed.

After the recent attempted robbery, Little Jack had had a glass screen installed in front of the counter. The last time I'd called in at the shop, he hadn't been able to hear me through the glass, but since then, he'd had an intercom installed.

I pressed the talk button. "If you don't mind me saying so, you're looking rather hot and bothered today, Jack."

"It's boiling hot in here, Jill. When the sun gets onto the glass, it's like a greenhouse."

"That explains the shorts and vest. Have you managed to solve the problem of scanning the goods yet?"

"I have indeed. I've come up with what I believe is a fantastic solution. I'm sure you'll be impressed." He pointed to a rack at the side of the counter.

"What are those?"

"Handheld scanners. Every time you put something into your shopping basket, you scan it with one of those, and when you're finished, you come back to the counter, press the buy button, and that will put the total up on the screen."

"Brilliant. I'll give it a go."

I grabbed one of the handheld devices and proceeded to pick up the bits and bobs I needed. As well as the bread and milk, I grabbed some muesli for Jack, and a packet of custard creams for me. Every time I put something into the basket, I scanned the barcode with the handheld device. It was all very easy.

When I'd finished, I went back to the counter.

"Okay, Jack, I've got everything I need. What do I do now?"

"Just press the green buy button on the handheld device."

"Okay, I've done that."

Jack checked his screen. "That will be fifty-five pounds and thirty-two pence, please."

I almost choked. "How much?"

"Fifty-five pounds and thirty-two pence."

"But I've only got these few bits and bobs. That can't possibly be right."

"According to my screen, you've bought two bottles of champagne and a pot of caviar."

"I think your new system might have a few teething problems, Jack."

***

Poor Little Jack. He wasn't having a great deal of luck with his shop at the moment. After the champagne and caviar debacle, he'd been forced to add up the items in my basket manually, and he'd promised to get someone in to sort out the scanning system.

I was just about to get into my car when I spotted an old lady on the pavement across the road. She was carrying a couple of heavy shopping bags and she seemed to be struggling a little. I was about to go over and offer her a hand when, suddenly, a young man on a bicycle came riding down the pavement at full speed. The old lady managed to get out of his way, but in doing so, she dropped both bags, and spilled the contents all over the ground. To my disgust, the young man just laughed and rode away. Still fuming at his inconsiderateness, I hurried across the road, and helped her to pick up her groceries and put them back into her bags.

"Thank you, young lady," she said in a feeble voice. "That's very kind of you."

"It's no trouble. Do you live far from here?"

"No, just around the corner."

"Let me carry these bags home for you."

"That's not necessary. I'm all right now."

I wasn't so sure about that; she still seemed quite shaken by the incident.

"I insist. Come on, I'll walk you home and take your shopping into the house."

Just as she'd said, she lived only a matter of minutes away. Once she'd unlocked the door, I carried the bags inside and put them onto the kitchen table.

"Thank you very much, young lady. I'm afraid I don't know your name."

"Jill. Jill Maxwell. Are you sure you're feeling all right? Is there someone I can call to come and be with you?"

"Certainly not." She waved away the suggestion. "I'm perfectly okay."

"Can I make you a cup of tea, at least?"

"That would be nice, but only if you join me."

"I'd love to."

"How rude of me. I haven't introduced myself. I'm Edith, Edith Petalwhite."

"It's lovely to make your acquaintance, Edith. Now, let me make that tea."

"I have some digestives if you'd like one." She pointed to the floral biscuit barrel.

"Not for me, thanks."

"They're chocolate."

"No, really. I'll be having my dinner shortly."

"Do you live around here, Jill?"

"Yes, just down the road."

"I didn't realise there were any witches in these parts."

Her remark caught me completely off guard. How on earth did she know I was a witch?

"I'm sorry," I said. "I didn't realise you were a sup."

"I'm a fairy godmother. Or, at least, I used to be. I'm retired now. It all got a little bit too much for me."

"How long have you lived here? In the human world, I mean."

"Most of my life."

For the next fifteen minutes, we talked about all sorts of things: my family, her family, and the work she used to do, which sounded quite fascinating.

"If you're sure you're all right, Edith, I suppose I'd better be making tracks."

"Yes, I'm fine. Thank you again for earlier."

"Don't mention it."

"Maybe you'll pop by and visit me again sometime. I don't get many visitors."

"I'd love to."

"Before you go, Jill, there's a little something I'd like to give you. Would you wait there a moment?"

"Err — okay." I assumed she was going to give me cake or something, but when she returned, she was holding a small ornamental trinket box.

"I'd like you to have this, Jill, as a token of my gratitude for your help."

"I couldn't possibly accept it."

"You must or I'll be offended. It doesn't have any value, but it's rather pretty, don't you think?" She handed it to me.

To be perfectly honest, it was one of the ugliest things I'd ever seen. "Yes, it's lovely. Thank you. That's very kind of you."

"I'm afraid I don't have the key for it; I lost it ages ago. Still, it's a lovely thing just to put on a shelf and admire."

"Absolutely. I'll do that as soon as I get home." That ugly thing was going straight into the spare bedroom.

I said my goodbyes to Edith, and then made my way back to the car.

Chapter 4

I was fast asleep when Jack woke me with a gentle nudge. I rolled over to check the time, and to my horror, found it was only six o'clock.

"What are you doing, Jack? Why did you wake me up at this hour?"

"Can't you hear that noise?"

"What noise?"

"It's a kind of flapping sound. And a sort of cooing."

"Are you kidding me? If it's flapping and cooing, then guess what? It's probably birds. They're always digging around in the guttering."

"It's more than just a couple of birds. Listen."

Fully awake now, I sat up in bed, and listened. He was right. That was way more noise than a couple of birds could have made.

"It sounds like it's coming from the back of the house." I yawned. "Go and take a look out of the window."

He walked out of the bedroom, and a couple of minutes later, shouted, "Jill, you'd better come and look at this."

"What is it?"

"Quick. Come here."

That man was determined to deprive me of a few more minutes of beauty sleep.

"What's so exciting that you couldn't have just told —" I stared out of the window, open-mouthed. I couldn't quite believe what I was seeing.

There, on the back garden, were hundreds of pigeons; you couldn't see the lawn for them. They were flapping their wings, fighting with one another, cooing, and doing something unmentionable all over our garden. We definitely wouldn't need to buy any fertiliser for a while.

"What do you reckon is going on, Jill?"

I shrugged, all innocent-like, but I had a horrible feeling I knew only too well what was going on. I wasn't about to tell Jack that the pigeon invasion was probably the fault of that stupid pigeon app. What had Winky done? He was supposed to have turned it off.

"Why don't you go and have your shower, Jack? I'll go outside and shoo them away."

"You shouldn't have to do that. I'll do it."

"No, it's okay. You have to be at work first. Go and have your shower."

"Okay, if you're sure."

As soon as he was in the bathroom, I threw on some clothes and hurried out to the back garden.

"Hey, you guys. What are you all doing here?"

A fat pigeon, at the front of the group, seemed to have nominated himself spokesman. "We followed the pigeon route finder app. It was set to global. Do you know who called us here?"

"I have no idea." I shrugged. "I don't know anything about a pigeon app."

"It must be faulty again." The fat pigeon sighed. "That thing is so unreliable. Do you know how many miles I've flown to get here today?"

"I'm really sorry for your inconvenience, but it has nothing to do with me."

"I'm going to leave a one-star review for that stupid app."

"You should definitely do that, but now it would probably be best if you all left."

Clearly annoyed by their wasted journeys, they were all moaning and groaning, but eventually, one by one, they took to the air and flew away.

"Jill? What on earth is going on?"

Oh bum!

"Morning, Britt."

"Good morning. What were all those pigeons doing in your garden?"

"I have absolutely no idea. Just one of those inexplicable things, I guess."

"But why were they only in your garden? There wasn't a single one in ours."

"That is rather strange, isn't it? Still, they've gone now."

"Yes, but have you seen the state of your lawn?" She pinched her nose and pulled a face. "It's covered in poop."

"I'll get Jack to sort that out."

After Britt had gone back into her house, I grabbed my phone, and tried to figure out how to switch off the stupid pigeon app, but it was far too complicated for me to understand, so I simply uninstalled it.

By the time I got back into the house, Jack had showered and dressed, and was in the kitchen.

"They've gone," I announced. "But the lawn is covered in pigeon poop."

"What are we going to do about that?"

"*We* aren't going to do anything. I did my bit by getting rid of the birds. *You* can sort out the poop."

"Gee, thanks."

"My pleasure."

"Don't you think it's rather strange that there were no

pigeons in the neighbours' gardens? I checked Britt and Kit's, and Tony and Clare's, and there wasn't a single pigeon in either of them."

"Just one of the many mysteries of life, I guess."

"While you were getting rid of the pigeons, Dad called."

"Is he okay?"

"To tell you the truth, he sounded down in the dumps. He's missing Mum something terrible."

"I thought he was doing okay?"

"So did I, but he was really miserable just now. I've asked him to come over on Saturday. I hope that's okay."

"Of course it is. I assume he'll stay the night?"

"No. I suggested that, but he didn't want to. He said he'd rather come first thing in the morning and leave late afternoon."

"Fair enough. Have you ever given any thought to whether he might benefit from seeing your mum again?"

"Not really. I'm not sure how Dad would react if I started to talk about Mum's ghost."

"Seeing her again might be just what he needs to cheer him up."

"I don't even know how I'd broach the subject with him. He'd probably think I'd lost my marbles."

"Why don't I nip over to GT today? I could have a chat with Yvonne. If she thinks it's a good idea, then it might be worth raising the subject with your dad."

"Okay. Why not?"

We'd finished breakfast, and I was busy loading the dishwasher.

"When are you going to CASS again, Jill?"

"Next week, on Wednesday, but I haven't even begun

to prepare the lesson yet. To be honest, I don't have a clue what I'm going to talk about."

"You'll come up with something; you always do. Have they got a new headmaster yet?"

"What makes you think it's going to be a head*master*? It might be another head*mistress*. But no, as far as I know, they haven't appointed anyone yet. I'll ask Ms Nightingale what's happening when I go over there next week."

"Oh, and by the way, Jill, whatever happened to the hobby you were supposed to be getting for yourself?"

"I've been too busy."

"Nonsense. You've had plenty of time to come up with something. Your problem is, you're all work and custard creams."

"Nonsense. I'll have myself a hobby before the end of the week."

"Promise?"

"Would I lie to you?"

***

When I stepped into my office building, I spotted a new sign on the wall at the bottom of the stairs. On it was a red arrow, pointing up the stairs, and below that were the words:

Clowns this way

What a cheek! Jimmy and Kimmy had obviously taken it upon themselves to put up the new sign without consulting me first. What would my clients think when they walked into the building, and saw a sign that informed them that the clowns were upstairs? This was unacceptable. I would have to have a word with those two.

Seeing the sign had reminded me that I should give Terry Tune a call, to find out where my sign was. I'd been waiting for that thing since forever. The last I'd heard, he was making yet another replacement because the last one had been installed upside down, and had broken in half when they'd tried to turn it around.

Mrs V was busy crocheting.

"Did you see the new sign downstairs, Mrs V?"

"The clown one? Yes. I didn't think you'd be very happy about it."

"You're dead right. I'm not. I'll have to have a word with Jimmy and Kimmy later. I think they've got a cheek."

"Did you ask Jack about dinner, Jill?"

"Sorry, he didn't get in until after I'd gone to bed last night, and then this morning, I'd intended to ask him, but we had a bit of a pigeon incident. I'll definitely ask him tonight."

"What kind of pigeon incident? Was it your neighbours' racing pigeons again?"

"Yeah, something like that. It's a long story. I don't want to bore you with it. Do you think you could make me a coffee?"

"Yes, dear, of course. I'll bring it through."

Winky was sitting on my desk, looking very pleased with life.

"Hey, I've got a bone to pick with you."

"Me?" He gave me that innocent look of his. "What

have I done now?"

"Do you remember yesterday when you said you'd turn off the pigeon app for me?"

"Yeah, what about it?"

"You didn't turn it off."

"Are you sure? I thought I had."

"Well, you were wrong. You set it to some kind of global call sign. This morning, Jack and I were woken by the sound of a thousand pigeons on our back garden."

Winky laughed so hard that he almost fell off the desk. "That's just too funny."

"I'm glad you think so because I certainly don't. The back garden is covered in pigeon poop."

"Stop it! Stop it!" He was holding his sides.

Five minutes later, Winky was still in hysterics when I rang Terry Tune.

"Sign Of The Times, Terry Tune, speaking."

"Terry, it's Jill Maxwell."

"Hello, Jill, how are you?"

"I'd be an awful lot better if I had my sign."

"I'm afraid I have good news and bad news about that."

Not for the first time during this escapade, my heart sank.

"The good news is that your replacement sign is ready."

"What's the bad news?"

"I'm afraid it's going to be a little while before we can install it."

"Why?"

"We're short-staffed, unfortunately. I do appreciate your patience, though."

"My patience ran out several weeks ago. Why haven't

you replaced the guy who won the lottery? It can't be that difficult."

"I did replace him, but the day after his replacement started, the new guy won half-a-million on a scratch card. He's resigned now too."

"That's just great."

"I am truly sorry, Jill, but it shouldn't be more than two weeks now, I promise."

***

After I'd finished my coffee, I magicked myself over to Cakey C in Ghost Town.

My mother was busy behind the counter. I say busy, but she was actually just standing around, talking to one of the customers. It was her assistant, Yvonne, who was doing all the work.

"Hello there, stranger." My mother gave me a little wave. "It's been a while since we've seen you over here. I thought you'd fallen out with us."

"I've been really busy. How's the shop doing?"

"Very well. As you can see, we're going from strength to strength."

"Mum, would you mind if I had a quick word with Yvonne in private?"

"I suppose so. You won't be too long though, will you? We're very busy this morning." She looked horrified at the thought of having to do some work herself.

"It'll only take a minute, I promise."

She turned to Yvonne. "Jill would like a word with you. Why don't you take your break now?"

I grabbed one of the tables at the back of the shop so

that we could talk without my mother eavesdropping.

"Is everything okay?" Yvonne said.

"Yes, Jack had a phone call from Roy this morning."

"Is he all right? There's nothing wrong is there?"

"No. At least, nothing physical. Jack said his dad seemed rather depressed. He got the impression that Roy's missing you."

"Oh dear. Poor Roy. He always did rather depend upon me."

"Jack and I were both wondering what you thought about making contact with Roy."

"I hadn't really considered it. He never had much time for ghosts and the supernatural. If I did manage to make contact, I'm worried it might upset or scare him."

"I definitely think it's worth some consideration. He's already depressed, so what do you have to lose? Knowing that you're still around might just lift his spirits." I laughed. "*Spirits*? Get it?"

She just gave me what I took to be a sympathetic look, but I continued anyway, "What do you think, Yvonne? Do you reckon it would be worth a try?"

"If both of you think it might do some good, then I'm happy to give it a go. I'd like nothing better than to see Roy and to talk to him again."

"Great. I'll tell Jack that you're okay with it. He'll have to see if he can persuade Roy to be open-minded enough to at least give it a try. Roy is coming over to our place on Saturday, so if he gives us the nod, you could try to make contact with him then."

"Okay. Will you let me know how Jack gets on?"

"Yes, of course."

I was about to leave when Yvonne caught hold of my

hand.

"Hold on a minute, Jill. I was actually going to contact you later today, to ask a favour."

"What can I do for you?"

"Madge Rumbelow, a friend of mine, has had some jewellery go missing from her house recently, and the police don't seem particularly interested. When she told me about it, I mentioned that you were a private investigator, and I said I thought you might be able to help. Do you think you could?"

"I'll be happy to try. If you let me have her details, I can pop over there in the next day or so."

Chapter 5

The Parkside Hotel's brochure described itself as a boutique hotel, but as far as I could see, it was nothing more than a glorified budget hotel.

The receptionist was too busy checking her Instagram to notice I was standing there.

"Yes, *madam*, how can I help you?"

"My name is Jill Maxwell. I'm a private investigator. I'd like to speak to someone about a man who disappeared from your hotel."

"I'm afraid you've made a mistake, madam. The man who disappeared recently didn't do so from this hotel."

"Actually, I'm not talking about the man who disappeared in the last week or so. I'm investigating a similar incident that happened over two years ago, and it was most certainly from this hotel."

"Oh? I didn't work here then."

"In that case, do you think I could speak to the manager?"

"I'm not sure he's available."

"Perhaps you could give him a ring and check?"

Rather reluctantly, she made the call. I couldn't hear what was being said, but judging by her expression, she was clearly surprised by the response.

"The manager will see you. He'll be down in a few minutes if you'd care to take a seat over there."

I'd no sooner sat down, than a tall man in a designer suit appeared in reception, and greeted me with a warm smile and a handshake.

"My name is Siegfried Topp, but everyone calls me Siggy. My receptionist tells me that you're interested in an incident that happened here a couple of years ago. A disappearance, I believe she said?"

"That's correct. I'm working for a lady called Lorraine Cross. Her brother disappeared from this hotel over two years ago. I wondered if you could tell me what you remembered about it?"

"I wish I could help, but unfortunately, I've only worked here for just over a year myself."

"Is there anyone else you can think of who would have been here back then?"

"Like most hotels, we have quite a high turnover of staff. However, I do know that the head of housekeeping, a lady named Denise Black, was working here then. She may remember something about the incident you mentioned."

"Would it be possible for me to speak to her?"

"Unfortunately, it's her day off today."

"Could you give me her phone number?"

"I'm not able to do that, I'm afraid, but if you leave me your card, I will speak to her and ask if she's prepared to talk to you. You must understand, though, if she'd prefer not to get involved, then I would have to respect her decision."

"That's fair enough. Thank you very much, Siggy. You're a star. And I'm not *dust* saying that."

***

The first thing I saw when I got back to my office building was that stupid sign. It was time I had a word with Jimmy and Kimmy, so I hurried up the stairs and took a left down the corridor to Clown. On reception,

Kimmy was dressed in full clown costume, as usual.

"Hi, Jill, how are you?"

"I'm a bit cheesed off to tell you the truth, Kimmy."

"It's Sneezy when I'm in costume."

"Whatever. I'm a bit cheesed off, *Sneezy*."

"What's the matter? I don't think I've ever seen you so angry. That whistling sound on the roof hasn't started up again, has it? I haven't heard anything in here."

"No, Sneezy, it's not the whistling sound. It's that sign at the bottom of the stairs."

"Our new one? Do you like it?"

"No, Sneezy, I most definitely do not."

"What's wrong with it?"

"The sign says that the clowns are upstairs."

"But that's correct. We *are* upstairs."

"Yes, but have you forgotten that my office is also up here?"

"I'm sure no one will get mixed up."

"Look at it this way, Sneezy. When a new client pays me a visit, I don't want the first thing they see to be a sign that says the clowns are upstairs. How do you think that would reflect on me?"

"I see what you mean. I hadn't thought about that. We certainly wouldn't want to do anything to upset you, Jill. You've been very kind to us. What do you suggest?"

If I'd been truthful in response to that question, I would have shocked her to the core. And besides, I wasn't sure it would have fitted anyway.

"You need to remove that sign and get a new one made."

"It was quite expensive, Jill."

"I'm the last person you should complain to about the

cost of signs. I've spent several weeks and a small fortune trying to get my own sign put up, and yet here I stand, still sans sign. I'm sure you'll manage to scrape together enough money to buy a new sign to go at the top of the stairs. And make sure it points down the corridor to the clown school. That way there should be no confusion."

"I'll have to talk to Breezy about it."

"Why don't you do that, and if he's got a problem, tell him to come and see me, would you?"

Mrs V was filing her nails. With her eyes closed.

"Mrs V?"

"Sorry, dear. I didn't see you standing there."

"Why did you have your eyes closed?"

"I can't bear to look at my nails while I'm filing them."

"Right? And why is that?"

"I've never been able to. It sends me all unnecessary. Doesn't it have that effect on you?"

"I just bite mine." Mrs V pulled a face, like I was the weird one. "I've just had a word with Kimmy about their new sign."

"How did that go?"

"She promised to talk to Jimmy. I suggested that they have a new sign installed at the top of the stairs. That way there'll be no confusion."

Winky was sitting on the windowsill, chatting to Harold. He had his back to me, and he began to laugh loudly.

"There were hundreds of them in her back garden. I wish I could have been there to see them."

I didn't need two guesses to know what he was

laughing at. He was no doubt telling Harold about the hordes of pigeons who had landed in my back garden.

Harold spotted me and waved a wing. "Hi, Jill. I'm really sorry to hear about what happened. It must've been a nightmare for you."

"It wasn't your fault, Harold. You weren't the one who set the app to global." I glared at Winky, who continued to laugh.

"Ida is really grateful for what you did, Jill. It's been a long time since she and Emma have had the chance to get together."

"No problem. It was my pleasure. How will Emma find her way back home with her terrible sense of direction?"

"Fortunately, a close neighbour of hers has the app too. When Emma decides to go home, her neighbour will set the app to give her directions. If there's ever anything that Ida or I can do for you, you really must let us know."

"Can you dispose of an unwanted cat?"

As always, Luther Stone arrived dead on time; the man was nothing if not punctual. He was looking particularly dapper, and he certainly seemed a lot happier than on his last visit.

"It's nice to see you again, Jill." He beamed. "I wasn't sure if I'd come to the right place."

"How do you mean?"

"Your sign has disappeared, and when I walked into the building, I saw a sign that said the clowns were upstairs."

"I've been having a few problems signage-wise recently. I'd rather not discuss it if you don't mind. I have to say, Luther, you're looking much happier than the last time you were here."

"That's because I am. I'm very pleased to say that I've found myself a new lady friend. Her name is Rebecca."

"That's great news. You deserve someone special. How did you meet her?"

"Through work; I do her books. She's a personal fitness instructor. Since the two of us got together, I've started working out more."

"I can tell. You're in great shape."

"Thanks. She and I really hit it off; we have loads in common. You, Jack, Rebecca and I should go out for dinner some time."

"I'd like that."

Luther had taken the paperwork through to the outer office. I was hopeful that, this time, he'd be able to report that everything was in order, and that there had been an upturn in business since his last visit.

A girl can hope, can't she?

Twenty-minutes later, he popped his head around the door. "Do you have a moment to answer a couple of questions, Jill?"

"Of course. What do you want to know?"

"It's about some of the expenses you've charged to the business. Do you remember the last time I went through your books? I said you needed to be very careful about what you included?"

"Yes, and I took you at your word. Everything on there is a genuine business expense."

"Right? Well, there are a couple of items that caught my eye. The first one is for a hundred balloons. Are they really a business expense?"

"*Balloons*? Actually, no, that shouldn't be in there. I

must've included that bill by mistake. The balloons were for Lizzie's birthday party."

"Okay, no problem. I'll scrap that one. And then there's just one other: You appear to have purchased some deep sea diver's boots?"

***

Foolishly, I'd allowed myself to hope that, after Luther had finished his review, he'd congratulate me on turning the business around. In fact, the words he used were *teetering on the edge.*

By the time he left, I was feeling rather despondent, and began to mutter to myself, "There's no justice. I work so hard."

"I guess it's only a matter of time, then," Winky said.

"What is?"

"Until this place goes to the wall. Where am I supposed to live then?"

"That's just typical of you. You're so selfish. What about me? How will I survive?"

"I hear they're looking for shelf stackers at the supermarket down the road at the moment."

"It won't come to that. I can still turn this business around."

"You know what you need, don't you?"

"I get the feeling you're about to tell me."

"I already have. My marketing expertise."

"That's where you're wrong. What I need is coffee and a blueberry muffin."

***

I magicked myself over to Cuppy C, in the hope that a latte and cake might make things look a little brighter. To my surprise, both of the twins were behind the counter.

"What are you doing here, Pearl? Isn't it your day off?"

"I only popped in for a few minutes to have a chat with Amber. Would you like to hear our good news?"

The way I was feeling, the last thing I needed was to hear someone else's good news, but I knew they were going to tell me anyway, so I said, "Yeah, sure."

"We've only gone and won the Candlefield Community monthly raffle," Pearl said.

"I wouldn't get too excited. Look what happened when I thought I'd won the Washbridge Lottery."

"Yes." Amber sniggered. "But you didn't actually know what your prize was, did you? You somehow managed to convince yourself that it was a car. We know exactly what we've won: it's a weekend for two at the Candlefield Country Park Hotel."

"Very nice. Which one of you won it?"

"We always said that if one of us won the raffle, we'd split the prize."

"But if it's a weekend for two, shouldn't one of you be taking your husband with you?"

"How can we do that if we're going to split the prize? We'll both be going. And besides, William and Alan love to look after the kids."

"Have you told them yet?"

"Not yet, but they'll be thrilled. And we'll be pampered all weekend long."

"That's fantastic." I sighed.

"Don't sound too enthusiastic, Jill. Why are you looking

so miserable anyway?"

"I'm not."

"Yes, you are. You look like a wet weekend."

"If you must know, I've just had a visit from my accountant."

"I take it that didn't go well."

"That would be the understatement of the year."

Chapter 6

Given their recent good fortune in the Candlefield raffle, and my bad news on the accounting front, I thought the twins might take pity on me, and let me have the coffee and muffin on the house. But they both scoffed at the suggestion, and said I should be grateful for my discount.

Those two were such tightwads.

I'd just finished my muffin when my phone rang. And, given the day I'd had so far, it was the last person I wanted to hear from.

"Hello, Grandma."

"I need you over at Ever right away."

"I'm rather busy just now."

"Eating a muffin in Cuppy C? I don't call that being busy." How did she know where I was and what I was doing? "I have something of the utmost importance that I need to discuss with you."

"Okay." I sighed. "I'll be over there in a couple of minutes."

I magicked myself to the alleyway close to Ever. As I walked up the high street, I noticed a couple of elderly gentlemen going into the shop.

Julie was on duty and she was wearing the awful canary yellow uniform.

"Hi, Jill, we haven't seen you in here for quite a while."

"To tell you the truth, I try to steer clear of this place if I can. How's business at the moment?"

"Going from strength to strength. Your grandmother is always coming up with some new initiative or other."

"I saw a couple of old guys come in here." I glanced around the shop, but I couldn't see them. "I wouldn't have thought they were your typical customer?"

Before Julie could respond, Grandma appeared, barefoot, in the doorway of her office. "I thought I heard your voice. Didn't I tell you this was urgent?"

"Sorry, Grandma. I'm coming."

Julie leaned forward and whispered. "She's been in a foul mood all day. I think her bunions have been playing up again."

"Thanks for the warning."

Grandma had both of her bare feet up on the desk.

"Can't you put your shoes on, Grandma?"

"No, I can't. My bunions have been giving me gyp all day. When you're as old as I am, young lady, you'll understand the meaning of pain, and then you won't be so quick to judge. Take a seat."

If I'd done as she asked, her feet would have been only inches from my face.

"Err — no, thanks. I prefer to stand."

"Please yourself. I called you here to make sure that you'll be at the broom flying practice on Saturday."

"I still don't think it's a good idea for me to be in the troupe, Grandma. You said yourself that I'm not very good. Why don't you give Dimples Lowe her place back?"

"Absolutely not. I've chosen my A-team, and you're in the starting line-up."

Great. "Okay, I'll be there on Saturday." I started for the door.

"Wait a minute, young lady, not so fast. There's something else I need to tell you. I have some very exciting news." Somehow, I doubted that. "I've just been notified by Candle TV that they intend to cover our first official display live."

"I thought we'd already given our first display."

"That doesn't count. That was just a stupid competition that Ma Chivers dreamed up. I'm talking about the first display that will feature the routines we choreographed ourselves."

"I'm surprised that Candle TV would be interested in something like that."

"That's because you don't seem to appreciate just how popular broom flying used to be. News of its revival has obviously sparked a lot of interest."

"Okay, is that everything?"

"No, it isn't. Seeing as we're going to be on TV, I've decided we need new uniforms."

"Can't we just wear the witch's outfits as usual?"

"They won't do. We need something much more spectacular." She took a few sheets of paper from a drawer and placed them on the desk. "Take a look at these sketches I've made. These should give you an idea of the sort of thing I have in mind."

They were all hideous, but I was too diplomatic (okay, scared) to say as much. "The colours are rather bright, Grandma. They're practically luminous."

"Exactly. Our display is scheduled to take place at dusk, so we have to make sure that the troupe will stand out on TV."

"If we wear any of these, we'll definitely do that."

***

After the day I'd just had, I needed something to take my mind off accounts and broom flying. Then I remembered what Jack had said about getting a hobby.

Maybe he was right, and what better hobby than decoupage? After all, if Mrs V and Winky could do it, I was sure I could.

For the last fifteen minutes, I'd been watching a beginner's guide to decoupage on YouTube.

"What's that you're watching?" Winky had jumped onto my desk, and he was trying to see what I was looking at.

"Never you mind." I nudged him gently back onto the floor. I didn't need him ridiculing me.

The tutor in the video was decorating a small photo frame, and by the time the lesson had finished, I was confident that I could produce something similar.

I should be able to get all the supplies I needed from the local arts and crafts shop. Once I had those, I'd go home, make the frame and present it to Jack. Not only would he be surprised that I'd taken up a hobby, but he'd be able to use the frame for one of his millions of ten-pin bowling photographs.

"I'm going home, Mrs V. I've had quite enough for one day."

"I take it the meeting with the accountant didn't go well?"

"Why would you think that? It was fine," I lied. "I'll see you in the morning."

I'd walked past Washbridge Art and Craft shop many times, but I'd never actually ventured inside. I was confident they would have everything I needed: a small photo frame, patterned paper, glue and a brush.

The woman behind the counter looked to be in her mid-fifties and had the face of a bulldog. Judging by the way she snapped at me, she had the temperament to match.

"How can I help you, madam?"

"I'm interested in purchasing some decoupage supplies."

"Would that be for a beginner, intermediate level or advanced?"

"Beginner, I suppose."

"What exactly do you need?"

"I've just been watching a video on YouTube. It was for —"

"*YouTube*?" She shook her head. "Goodness me. That's entirely unsuitable. Who knows what qualifications if any, those people have?"

There are decoupage qualifications?

"We carry a wide range of approved how-to books. You'd be much better off following the instructions in one of those."

I glanced over at the shelves of books; the cheapest one was twenty-five pounds. Stuff that for a game of soldiers.

"I don't think I'll bother with a book, thanks."

"Suit yourself, but don't say I didn't warn you."

"All I need is a small photo frame and some patterned paper to decorate it with. I assume you have a selection I can look at? Oh, and glue and a brush."

"Very well, madam. Follow me." She led the way to the aisle where all the decoupage products were kept.

After I'd picked out the decorative paper, she priced it all up.

"So, that's the photo frame, the paper, the decoupage glue and brush. That comes to a grand total of forty-two pounds and thirty-six pence."

I almost fell over. I'd been expecting to pay no more than ten pounds.

"Would madam like a carrier bag?"

"Actually, I'm going to have to leave this lot for now."

"But what about the items you've already picked out?"

"Sorry. I've just remembered that there's somewhere I need to be. I'll probably pop back again tomorrow when I have more time."

There was no way I was going to spend that kind of money, and besides, I'd just remembered the small hardware shop, which was four doors down from Kathy's Bridal Shop. They were bound to have everything I needed.

Washbridge Knick-Knacks was an old-fashioned shop which sold everything from nails to rotovators (whatever they are). I'd no sooner walked through the door, than a slight man, dressed in a brown smock, came scurrying over to me.

"Hello, young lady. What are you looking for?"

"I need a small photo frame, some fancy wrapping paper and glue."

"You'll find the photo frames in aisle B. It's aisle G for the wrapping paper, and aisle J for the glue."

"Great, thanks."

"If you need any help, just give me a shout. My name is Andy. Andy Mann."

Of course it is. "Thanks, Andy."

I grabbed a basket, and in no time at all, had the photo

frame and decorative paper. I'd picked one which had pictures of bowling balls and skittles on it. That just left the glue. There were so many different kinds, and I had no idea which one would be most suitable. In the end, I figured the best thing to do was to get the strongest one, so I picked up a tube of superglue. Even better, I could apply it straight from the tube, so I wouldn't need to buy a brush.

The whole lot came to just over seven pounds. What a bargain!

***

When I arrived home, I laid out my supplies on the kitchen table. Carefully following the instructions from the YouTube demo, I placed the photo frame onto the decorative paper, and then cut the paper to size. Next, I had to fold the paper over the frame and glue it in place. After applying the glue to the frame, I turned down the paper and pressed it to the wood. Then I turned the frame over and did the same on the other side.

That was it. The whole thing had taken me less than five minutes. This decoupage stuff was easy. I couldn't understand what all the fuss was about.

After admiring my handiwork for a few minutes, I nipped upstairs to the loo. As I was leaving the bathroom, I could hear Jack moving around downstairs; he was shouting something, but I couldn't make out what, so I hurried back downstairs.

"Jill, what's this?" He was staring at the photo frame.

"This, Jack, is my new hobby. The one you said I would

never take up. But, as you can see, you were wrong because I am now a decoupage master. What do you think of the photo frame I made for you? Do you like it?"

"It's very nice, but there's one slight problem."

"The size, you mean? Surely you must have a photograph that will fit it."

"It's not that. Why don't you try to pick up the frame?"

I had no clue what he was getting at, but I did as he said. At least, I tried to, but it wouldn't budge.

"That isn't supposed to happen."

"What kind of glue did you use, Jill?" I glanced across at the kitchen worktop. "Don't tell me you used superglue."

"Err — actually, yeah."

"You do realise that this photo frame is never coming off this table, don't you?"

"Don't be ridiculous."

Jack loved to exaggerate. How difficult could it be? It was only a bit of glue after all.

"Leave it with me, Jack. I'll sort it out."

"Okay, good luck with that. I'm going to nip to the corner shop because I'm out of Garibaldi biscuits."

"Why do you insist on eating those horrible things when you could eat custard creams?"

"Are you offering?"

"Not *my* custard creams, obviously, but you could buy some of your own."

"I'll stick to Garibaldi if it's all the same to you."

Freak.

An hour later, we were seated at the kitchen table, eating dinner.

"Didn't I tell you that I'd get that photo frame off the table?"

"You certainly did." He raised his eyebrows. "But now we have a square ridge in the table where the frame used to be."

"I think it's what people call a design feature."

"I think it's what most sane people would call a mess."

"But you like your photo frame, don't you?"

"Yeah, it's lovely, but by the time we've forked out for a new kitchen table, it'll probably be the world's most expensive photo frame." Some people are just never grateful. "By the way, Jill, I talked to Dad earlier today and asked him about Mum."

"How did that go?"

"Not well, to be honest. As soon as I mentioned the subject of the afterlife, he started to get upset and said that I was talking nonsense."

"Oh dear. Do you still think it's worth Yvonne coming over here on Saturday?"

"Yeah, I think so. I don't see what we have to lose. Maybe once Dad's here, I'll be able to persuade him to be a little more open-minded."

"Okay. I'll update Yvonne but I'd better warn her there may still be some resistance from him."

"Great. By the way, Jill, when you last went to the corner shop, did they have those handheld scanners?"

"Yeah, they did. Has Little Jack got them sorted out yet?"

"I don't think so. All I did was buy a packet of Garibaldi biscuits, and he tried to charge me thirty-four pounds."

Chapter 7

The next morning, Jack had to leave for work early, so I skipped breakfast and called in at Coffee Games on my way into the office. At first, I thought there was no one behind the counter, and I was just about to call for service when Piers jumped up and almost scared me to death.

"Piers, what do you think you're playing at?"

"Sorry, Jill. It's hide and seek day."

"You should post a warning sign on the door. Can I get a caramel latte, please?"

"Of course. No muffin today?"

"No, thanks. Just the coffee."

"Do you want it to go, Jill?"

"No, I'm going to spend a few minutes in here before I go to the office."

Once I had my coffee, I started towards a table by the door, but then someone called my name.

"Morning, Daze. You've made an early start."

"Come and join me. We've got a lot of work on at the moment, so we thought we'd grab a coffee to give us a boost before we get started."

I glanced at the table and noticed there were two coffee cups. "Is Blaze with you?"

"Yes, he is." She grinned. "He's hiding."

"Aren't you supposed to be looking for him?"

"I suppose I am." She laughed. "Sooner or later, he'll realise that I'm not. Where's your blueberry muffin?"

"I don't always have a muffin."

"I've never seen you without one."

"Cheek. What is it that's keeping you two so busy?"

"We're on the lookout for a couple of rogue werewolves

on the loose here in Washbridge."

"How do you mean, *rogue*? What have they done?"

"Last time they were here, they attacked a number of humans."

"*Last time?*"

"Yes, they were recently released from Candlefield prison, after a long stretch inside. They should have been tagged to prevent them from coming over here, but some idiot forgot to do it. We were only alerted late yesterday."

"Have there been any attacks that you know of? I haven't seen anything in the newspaper."

"Nothing yet, thank goodness."

"Is there anything I can do to help?"

"Not really, but if you hear of anything unusual happening around Washbridge, give us a shout, would you?"

"Will do."

Just then, my phone rang.

"Is that Jill Maxwell?"

"Yes, Jill Maxwell speaking."

"This is Denise Black. I work at Parkside Hotel. The manager told me that you wanted to talk to me about the man who disappeared from the hotel a couple of years ago."

"That's right, Denise. Is there any chance we could get together for a few minutes sometime today?"

"I take my break at about eleven. It's only fifteen minutes, though. Will that be long enough?"

"More than enough, thanks."

"Okay. I'll wait for you in reception at eleven."

"Great. I'll see you then."

I'd just finished on the call when Blaze appeared

looking none too pleased with life.

"What's going on, Daze?" He snapped. "You were supposed to be looking for me?"

"Oh, yes," she said, straight-faced. "I knew there was something I'd forgotten to do."

***

When I arrived at my office building, I was pleased to see that the Clown sign had been removed from the bottom of the stairs. It seemed that Jimmy and Kimmy had taken my grievances seriously.

"Morning, Mrs V."

"Good morning, Jill. Did you ask Jack about dinner?"

Oh bum!

"I'm really sorry, Mrs V, but I forgot again."

"If you'd rather not come, just say. I won't be offended."

"No, it's not that, honestly. You know what my memory is like. I promise I'll ask him tonight. Cross my heart."

There was no sign of Winky in my office, but I could hear his voice coming from behind the screen; he appeared to be talking to himself.

"This is Winky FM, broadcasting to felines across the UK. Stay tuned for the country's coolest sounds."

Huh?

I popped my head around the screen and discovered that he'd set up what looked like a mini sound studio. He was wearing a pair of headphones and was speaking into a microphone.

"The best of the feline charts is right here every day. And now, something that will get you dancing. One of my favourites: Mouser and the Trapbusters." He threw a switch on the console in front of him.

I tapped him on the shoulder. "What's going on here?"

He pulled off the headphones. "What does it look like?"

"It looks like you're running a radio station out of my office."

"Correct. This, Jill, is Winky FM."

"You can't run a radio station from in here."

"I already am."

"Don't you need a licence to do this kind of thing?"

"Pah, that's just red tape. You worry way too much, Jill. Oh, and by the way, how did your attempt at decoupage go?"

How on earth did he know about that?

"I don't know what you're talking about."

"Yes, you do. You were looking at the beginner's guide to decoupage on YouTube."

"How do you know that?"

"Because, after you'd left yesterday, I checked your browser history."

"You had no right to do that."

"So, how did it go? What did you make?"

"I didn't make anything. I only watched the video out of curiosity."

"You made a mess of it, didn't you? Come on, tell me. What happened? You should bring it in to show me. I could do with a good laugh."

***

Siegfried Topp, the manager of the Parkside Hotel, had kindly agreed to allow me to speak to Denise Black in his office.

"Thanks for agreeing to talk to me Denise."

"That's okay. I'm happy to help if I can."

"I take it you remember the incident I'm investigating? The disappearance of a man from this hotel a couple of years ago?"

"Yes, I do. The first time I saw him was shortly after he'd checked in. I remember because I was walking down the corridor when I tripped and dropped a pile of towels onto the floor. Most guests would have just walked on by, but he stopped and helped me to pick them up. He was a real gentleman."

"And you say that was shortly after he checked in?"

"Yes. He had his case with him and was on his way to his room."

"How did he seem?"

"Fine. Once he knew I was okay, we both had a laugh at my mishap."

"You said that was the first time you saw him. I take it from that you saw him again?"

"That's right. Later that same day. He was coming out of his room with a woman."

"I see. Had they booked in as a couple?"

"No, but that's not particularly unusual." She smiled. "That kind of thing happens a lot."

"And was that the last time you saw him?"

"Yes. The next morning, the girl who'd been assigned to clean his room, came to tell me that it didn't look as though anyone had spent the night in there. She wanted to know whether she still needed to clean it or not."

"Isn't that a little unusual?"

"A little, but it's not totally unheard of. Sometimes

people have one drink too many somewhere else and don't make it back to the hotel. It does happen from time to time."

"What happened next?"

"He should have checked out the following day, but he never did. His case and all his clothes were still in his room."

"What about his bill?"

"He'd paid for the room in advance, and he hadn't had any room service, or meals in the restaurant, so there was nothing additional to pay."

"What do you do with a guest's belongings when something like that happens?"

"We hold them somewhere safely until such time as the guest returns to claim them, but in this case, that never happened. He never came back."

"Was that a first?"

"The only other time I remember it happening was when a guest skipped out without paying."

"I assume the police paid a visit to the hotel after the man's disappearance was reported?"

"Yes, but not until some time afterwards. Before that, we had a visit from his wife who came looking for him."

"Was that the same woman you'd seen him with earlier?"

"No, it wasn't."

***

Back at the office, Winky was still behind the screen, playing at being a DJ. Thankfully I couldn't hear the music, but I did have to put up with his inane patter.

"Fans of Winky FM, do I have a special treat for you. Tomorrow I'll be interviewing Washbridge's leading authority on decoupage. Yes, you heard it right. I will be talking to none other than Jill Maxwell."

I jumped out of my chair and rushed behind the screen.

"I'm not going on your stupid radio show!"

He pulled off his headphones and laughed. "Relax, I'm not even on air at the moment. I was only winding you up. And besides, my listeners are way too cool for decoupage."

"I'm not in the mood for your practical jokes. They're not the least bit funny."

"Maybe not, but I bet whatever you tried to decoupage yesterday was hilarious. Come on Jill, you have to bring it in for me to see."

"I've already told you. I didn't make anything."

"If you won't bring it in, will you at least take a photo of it?"

"There's nothing to take a photo of."

"I know you're lying. I'll make it my business to find out what you made."

"How do you intend to do that?"

"So you admit there is something?"

"What? No, I don't! And I don't want to hear another word about decoupage. It's a stupid hobby, anyway."

A few minutes later, Mrs V popped her head around the door.

"Your brother's here. He wondered if you could spare him a minute."

I hadn't been expecting a visit from Martin. In fact, I'd been under the impression that he'd gone away for the week.

"Okay, send him in, please."

He walked into the office, carrying the largest bouquet of flowers I'd ever seen.

"Hi, Martin. I didn't think you were in Washbridge this week."

"I'm here, but I'll be tied up in the evenings. That's why I couldn't meet up with you and Kathy until next week. You don't mind me popping in like this, do you?"

"Actually Martin, and I don't mean to be rude, I am rather busy at the moment. It would have been better if you'd called in advance."

"Sorry, Jill. It's just that I'm still excited at the idea of having a sister." He handed me the flowers. "These are for you."

"Thanks, they're beautiful."

He hesitated, then said, "I might be picking up the wrong signals, but I get the feeling you're still a little uneasy about our relationship. It's almost as though you don't trust me."

"Okay, let me put my cards on the table. Until recently, I didn't even know you existed. And although I'm really pleased that you're in my life now, I do think that you need to dial it back a little. It's all a bit too much for me."

"You're right. I'm sorry. I'll get going. I can see you're busy."

"Hang on. I'm the one who should be sorry. I shouldn't have said that."

"No, you were right. I've been coming on way too strong. I'll see you next week." And with that, he left.

I was still staring at the door when Winky popped his head around the screen.

"How could you treat your long-lost brother like that?"

"He caught me off guard. I wasn't expecting him to call in like that."

"And he bought you flowers, too. What a horrible person he is."

"Stop it, Winky. I feel bad enough already. There's no need for you to stick the boot in."

"He does look like you, though. Tough break."

Just then, Mrs V walked into the office. "Is your brother all right, Jill? He was really bubbly when he arrived, but just now, when he left, he looked quite upset."

Oh bum!

I was still feeling guilty about the way I'd treated Martin, when I magicked myself over to GT. At the request of Yvonne, I was going to talk to Madge Rumbelow.

You know those charming little cottages that you see on the lids of biscuit tins at Christmas? Well, Madge's cottage was nothing like that. The place was practically falling to pieces: The thatched roof had holes in it, the garden was overgrown, and the window frames looked like they hadn't seen a lick of paint for decades. I tried to knock by using the metal doorknocker, but it seemed to have rusted closed, so I had to hammer on the door with my hand. After a few moments, a lovely old lady with red cheeks and bright blue eyes came to the door.

"Yes, young lady. What can I do for you?"

"Are you Mrs Rumbelow?"

"That's right. Who are you, dear?"

"My name is Jill Maxwell. Yvonne, who works at Cakey C, asked me to come and see you."

"You must be the private investigator lady. Do come inside. You'll have to excuse the place, it's a little untidy at the moment."

That was something of an understatement. The house wasn't dirty—in fact, it appeared to be spotlessly clean, but it was incredibly untidy. There were piles of papers, numerous boxes, and all manner of things in the hallway. And the lounge was pretty much the same. It was hard to imagine how anyone managed to clean around the piles of junk.

"Find a seat, if you can," she said. "I've been meaning to tidy up for a couple of days."

Couple of days? Couple of years more like.

"I'll go and make us a nice cup of tea. How do you take yours? Sorry, I've forgotten your name."

"It's Jill. Milk with two-thirds spoonfuls of sugar, please."

"Right you are, and please call me Madge." She disappeared out of the room, and I could hear pots clattering in the kitchen. A couple of minutes later she came back. "I'm sorry, dear. Did you say you do take milk?"

"Yes, please."

"And no sugar, wasn't it?"

"Just a little sugar, please."

She scuttled off again, and a couple of minutes later came back, carrying a tray with just one cup on it.

"I'm sorry, dear, I seem to have forgotten your drink." Once again, she scooted back into the kitchen. When she returned, she handed me a cup of tea, which clearly had no milk in it.

"Thank you, Madge." I took a sip, and it was so sweet

that it was undrinkable. She must have put half a packet of sugar in it.

"I'm sorry, I don't have any biscuits, Jean. I seem to have misplaced them."

"It's Jill, and don't worry about it. The tea's fine. Yvonne tells me that you've had some jewellery go missing."

At this point, I was beginning to wonder if the jewellery really had gone missing or if she'd just misplaced it amongst all the jumble.

"That's right. Two items, actually."

"Is it possible you could have misplaced them, Madge?"

"Absolutely not. I keep all my jewellery in the jewellery box."

"Okay. Would you describe them to me?"

After she'd done that, I continued, "Was there any sign of a break-in?"

"No, nothing at all."

"What about visitors? Do you have many?"

"My family of course. And then there's Mrs Grimes."

"Who's she?"

"The cleaner. She comes in about once a fortnight."

Mrs Grimes certainly earned her money having to clean that place.

"Any other visitors, Madge?"

"There's Mr Green. He's the gardener, but he rarely comes inside the house."

"Do you think you could let me have contact details for Mrs Grimes and Mr Green?"

"Yes, dear. I'll go and jot them down for you now."

Chapter 8

I made my way to 47 Poltergeist Road, the home of Mrs Grimes, Madge's cleaning lady. I was intrigued to meet the woman who was somehow able to keep Madge's house so clean, despite the fact there was junk piled up all over the place.

I knocked on the door, but there was no response; she was probably out cleaning someone else's house. I gave it one more try, and this time I heard footsteps inside.

"Hello? Who's that?" A female voice came from the other side of the door.

"Hi. My name is Jill Maxwell. Is that Mrs Grimes?"

"Yes. What do you want?"

"I believe you clean house for Madge Rumbelow?"

She opened the door slowly. "That's right. I do. Are you looking for someone to clean your house?"

"Actually, no. I was hoping for a few minutes of your time to discuss Madge."

"What about her?"

"I don't know if you're already aware, but she's had a few items of jewellery go missing recently."

"If you think I've stolen them, you're badly mistaken," she snapped. "I'm as honest as the day is long. You can ask any of my customers."

"No, you've got the wrong idea. I'm not here to accuse you of anything. I'd just like to ask you a few questions."

"I can't talk for long. I'm due at my next job in a few minutes."

"Of course. I understand. How often do you clean for Madge?"

"Once a fortnight. Every other Friday."

"It can't be an easy house to clean. There's so much clutter in there."

"Tell me about it. It takes much longer than it should do."

"Still, you make a very good job of it. As far as I could see, the house was spotless."

"Yes, well, I take great pride in my work. You can ask any of my clients."

"I believe you. Anyway, as I was saying, Madge has had some jewellery go missing, and as you'd expect, she's quite upset."

"I don't blame her. I would be too. Ghost Town never used to be like this, you know. There was a time when you could leave your door open and not have to worry about it. Those days are gone, I'm afraid."

"Quite. While I was with Madge, I couldn't help but notice that she is a little bit forgetful."

"You're right there." Mrs Grimes smiled for the first time. "Madge is a darling, but her memory isn't what it used to be."

"Do you think it's possible that she might have misplaced the jewellery?"

"Anything's possible in that house, but if she'd left it lying around, I would probably have seen it."

"What about visitors to the house? Does she have many, would you know?"

"Not that I've seen, but then I'm only there for a few hours every two weeks."

"Do you think it's possible someone could have distracted her at the door while someone else sneaked inside?"

"It's certainly possible. Madge is easily distracted as

you've probably noticed." Mrs Grimes checked her watch. "I'm sorry, but I really must get going now or I'll be late for my next job."

"Okay. Thanks for your help." I handed her my card. "If you think of anything else that might help, please call me."

My next port of call was at the home of Mr Green, Madge Rumbelow's gardener. There was no response when I knocked on the door of his flat, and I was just about to walk away when one of his neighbours poked his head out of the door.

"Are you looking for Arthur?"

"Mr Green? Yes. You wouldn't happen to know where he is, would you?"

"He'll be at work."

"Right. I'll have to call back later. Do you know what time he usually gets home?"

"Any time between five and seven. Mind you, he always works at Ghost Town Park on a Wednesday. You might catch him there if it's urgent."

"Thanks very much. I'll give it a go."

I'd never been to Ghost Town Park before, but it was simple enough to find, and much larger than the ones in Candlefield. Barry would have loved it.

It took me quite a while to track down Mr Green who I eventually found weeding the flower beds at the far side of the park.

"Mr Green?" I gave him a little wave.

"That's me."

"I wonder if you could spare me a few minutes?"

"I can always find time for a pretty young lady."

"Thanks. I believe you work for Madge Rumbelow."

"I do indeed. I visit her every three weeks, just to tidy her garden. It isn't a big job; it doesn't take very long. Is she all right?"

"Madge is fine. My name is Jill Maxwell. I'm a private investigator."

"A private investigator, eh? I'm not in any trouble, am I?"

"No, nothing like that. Madge has had some jewellery go missing recently, so I'm talking to everyone who visits her house."

"I see. Well I can promise you that I didn't take it." He grinned. "I don't think her jewellery would suit me, do you?"

"I'm sure you didn't. I just wondered if you'd seen anyone visit her house while you were working there? Anyone suspicious?"

"I can't say that I have." He hesitated. "Wait a minute, though. Now I come to think of it, I did see a white van parked out the front of her house last week while I was there. It was only there for a few minutes."

"You don't happen to know who it was, do you?"

"No, I'm sorry. I have no idea."

"Okay, well thank you for your time. I mustn't keep you from your work."

"No problem, young lady. I hope you find Madge's jewellery."

I was curious to find out more about the white van, so I made my way back to Madge's house. When I got there, I was rather surprised to find her in a bit of a flap.

"Is everything all right, Madge?"

"I'm supposed to be going to the bridge club, but my lift has let me down. I'll never get there on time if I take the bus."

"I don't have a car, but I could magic you there if you'd be okay with that?"

"Yes please, Jill. I'd really like that. I just need to go and get my bag from the bedroom. I'll only be a minute."

While she was upstairs, I noticed a photograph on the sideboard. I was still looking at it when she came back downstairs.

"That's my daughter, Cynthia. She's very pretty, isn't she?"

"She certainly is. Is she still in the human world?"

"Yes. I've tried to contact her several times, but I'm afraid she doesn't believe in ghosts. I really do miss her. I'd give anything to be able to speak to her again." A lump came to her throat, and I thought for a minute that she was about to cry, but she took a deep breath and managed to compose herself. "We'd better get going or we won't make it."

"Take my hand. Are you ready?" She nodded, and I magicked us both over to the bridge club.

"Do come inside, Jill. I'd like to introduce you to some of my friends."

"I really should get going."

"Please, just for a minute. They'd love to meet you."

"Okay then, but only for a minute."

Once we were inside, Madge took me over to meet an elderly lady in crumpled tights.

"This is Selina Mowbray, Jill. She's the organiser of the bridge club."

"I'm very pleased to meet you, Selina."

"Likewise, I'm sure."

Selina didn't look very pleased to meet me, and she made the first excuse she could to scuttle away.

"Look, over there. That's my friend, Lily." Madge beckoned to the woman who was standing near the window. "Lily, this is Jill. She's helping me to find my jewellery."

"It's very nice to meet you, Jill." Lily, at least, seemed sincere.

"I'll go and get some drinks," Madge said. "Would you like one, Jill?"

"Not for me, thanks. I'll have to be going in a minute."

While Madge was fetching the drinks, Lily said in a hushed voice, "You realise it's possible that Madge may have misplaced her jewellery, I assume? She's always forgetting things."

"Do you really think so?"

"Definitely. I lost some of my jewellery recently too, but I'm sure it'll turn up. Madge could easily have put it down somewhere and forgotten all about it. Don't tell her I said so, though, will you?"

"Of course not."

When Madge returned with the drinks, I asked if she'd be okay for getting back home.

"Yes, thank you, dear, I'll be able to get a lift. Thank you so much for bringing me."

"My pleasure. Before I go, can I ask you about the white van that was parked in front of your house last week while Arthur Green was there? Do you remember who it belonged to?"

"Let me think." She scratched her chin. "Oh yes, I

remember. It was the fish man."

"Do you have fish delivered to your door?"

"No. To tell you the truth, I'm not really a big fan of fish. The young man was going door-to-door to see if anyone was interested in having fish delivered. I told him that I wasn't, but he left me one of his cards anyway."

"I don't suppose you happen to have it with you, do you?"

"I think I put it in my handbag. Let me see. Yes, here it is."

I stared at it in disbelief. It read:
Terry Salmon, fish delivered to your door

I was in a state of shock when I left the bridge club. Could it really be the same Terry Salmon who delivered our fish? I tried to remember when we'd last had a fish delivery, and it was several weeks ago. In fact, Jack had said something the other day about being low on haddock. My curiosity was piqued, so I looked up the address on the card. It wasn't very far away, so I decided to find out what was going on.

When I arrived at the address, the white van was parked on the road, so I walked up the path, and knocked on the door. A few moments later, who should appear at the door but Terry Salmon.

I'm not sure which one of us was more shocked.

"Terry, it *is* you."

"What are you doing here, Jill? I didn't realise you'd died."

"I haven't."

"It's okay. I was in denial too when it happened to me, but I've sort of accepted it now. It would be much better if you could come to terms with it too."

"Honestly, Terry, I'm not dead."

"Then how come you're here in Ghost Town?"

"It's quite complicated. The thing is, I'm a witch."

He laughed. "There's no such thing."

"Actually, there is. I can use magic to travel back and forth between the human world, the paranormal world, and here in Ghost Town."

"Really? That's amazing. There are a few people I didn't get the chance to say goodbye to. Would you be able to use magic to take me back to the human world so I could do that?"

"I'm sorry, Terry, but that's impossible. I assume you're aware that you can make yourself visible to people in the human world?"

"So I've been told, but I wouldn't know where to start."

"I have a few friends here. I'm sure one of them would be able to help. I'll have a word with the colonel and ask him to make contact with you."

"That would be great, Jill. That's really kind of you."

"What happened to you, anyway? How did you die?"

"It was my own stupidity." He shook his head at the memory. "I had a walk-in freezer where I kept all of my stock. The emergency lock-release on the inside had been playing up for a few weeks, but instead of doing the sensible thing and getting it repaired, I just ignored it. I'd gone into the freezer to grab some haddock, and the door closed behind me. The emergency lock wouldn't budge, and of course no one knew I was in there."

"Oh dear. So you froze to death?"

"Yes, and I most definitely wouldn't recommend it."

"You certainly haven't wasted any time setting up

business here in Ghost Town."

"I thought it might help to take my mind off things. What will you do for fish now, Jill? Now that I've gone?"

"I don't know. I'm going to have to break the bad news to Jack."

***

When I got back to the house, I was quite surprised to find that Jack was already there.

"How come you're home so early?" I said.

"I was working on a case just outside Washbridge, so it wasn't worth going back to the station. I'm making spaghetti bolognese. Is that okay?"

"Sounds good to me."

Just then, there was a knock at the door.

"Good afternoon, madam." The man standing there was wearing white dungarees and a white flat cap. "My name is Harry Hart."

"Let me stop you right there, Mr Hart." I put up my hand. "I'll save us both some time. We never buy at the door."

By now, Jack was standing by my side.

"I'm not selling anything," he insisted. "I'm a window cleaner. My business is called Hart of Glass. Get it? *Hart of glass*?" He laughed. So did Jack, but then Jack would laugh at anything. "I wondered if you might be interested in having your windows cleaned?"

"How much does it cost, Mr Hart?" I asked.

"Ten pounds, and I come around every three weeks."

"You're in luck, then," I said. "I hate cleaning the windows. You can sign us up."

"Great. I'll be over here to do my first clean next week."

"Excellent. We'll see you then."

As soon as he'd left, Jack gave me one of those looks of his.

"What's wrong?" I said.

"What do you mean *you* hate cleaning the windows? You *never* clean the windows. I always do them."

"In that case, you should be thanking me."

Later, at the kitchen table, Jack was pushing the food around on his plate, without actually eating much of it.

"What's wrong? Have you lost your appetite?"

"To tell you the truth, I had my heart set on a bit of haddock tonight, but when I checked the freezer, we were all out."

"That reminds me. I'm afraid you're going to have to find a new fish man."

"Don't tell me Terry Salmon has packed it in."

"He's retired, I'm afraid. From life."

"What do you mean?"

"I was in Ghost Town earlier today, working on a case, and guess who I ran into?"

"Not Terry, surely."

"Yes, I'm afraid so."

"That's awful. He was so young. What happened?"

"Apparently, he locked himself in a freezer."

"What a horrible way to go."

"It makes me shudder just to think about it."

"That's not funny, Jill."

"So why are you laughing?"

Chapter 9

Have you ever had one of those mornings when your body is awake, but your mind is still fast asleep? Me too, and this was definitely one of them. It took all my strength just to shovel the cornflakes into my mouth.

Meanwhile, and annoyingly, Jack was wide awake and full of beans.

"Jill, you never told me how you went on with the accountant."

"I thought I had."

"No, you definitely didn't. So how did it go?"

"Okay."

"Is that okay *good* or okay *bad*?"

"It's just okay."

"What did Luther actually say?"

"That everything was okay." It was definitely time to change the subject. And quickly. "By the way, Jack, did I mention that I've landed a case similar to the one you're working on at the moment?"

"Vandalism in the toilet blocks at the school?"

"What? No, not vandalism in the toilet block. Didn't you say something about a man who had disappeared from a hotel in West Chipping?"

"Oh yeah, that's right. We haven't made much progress on that up to now. In fact, we've hit a bit of a brick wall. So, what is it that you're working on?"

"It's a cold case. I'm trying to find out what happened to a guy who disappeared from a hotel in Washbridge two years ago. Nobody's seen or heard from him since. His sister came to see me on Monday."

Just then, there was a knock at the door.

"Who's that at this time in the morning?" I dragged myself off the chair. "It had better not be Mr Hosey or I'll swing for him."

Unsurprisingly, given my condition, Jack beat me to the door. I recognised the man standing outside, but I couldn't think where I knew him from.

"You probably don't remember me," he said. "I'm Billy Bass. I called to see you some time ago to ask if you were interested in having fish delivered to your door. Back then, you said you had it covered. This is just a follow-up, to see if things have changed at all."

"Actually," Jack said, "we've just lost our regular fish supplier. He died recently."

"You must mean poor Terry Salmon. So tragic, and such a young man. It's hard to know what to say at times like this, isn't it? So, can I sign you up?"

Before Jack could respond, I grabbed his arm. "Excuse us for a minute, would you, Mr Bass?" When we were in the kitchen, I said to Jack in a whisper, "This guy is a vulture. Terry's barely cold in his grave."

"He died in a freezer. I suspect he's stone cold." Jack grinned.

"And you had the nerve to have a go at me for making jokes in bad taste."

"You're right. Sorry."

"We should tell this guy to sling his hook."

"If we do that, I'll have no fish. Are you volunteering to go to the fishmongers every week?"

"I most certainly am not. That place smells awful."

"In that case, I'm going to sign up with Mr Bass." Jack went back to the door. "Yes, we'd like to sign up."

I watched in disgust as Jack gave Billy (AKA Mr Jump

In Your Grave) Bass his order.

"Terry's tragic accident must have done wonders for your business," I sniped.

"It really has. In fact, I'm looking for an assistant to help with the additional work. You wouldn't be interested, would you?"

"Me?" I shuddered at the thought. "No, thank you."

"It's just that you have the look of someone who knows their way around fish. If you hear of anyone who's looking for a job, send them my way, would you?"

***

When I arrived at the office, Mrs V was holding a sheet of A4 paper, and had a confused look on her face.

"Oh dear, Jill." She sighed. "I really don't know what to say."

"About what? What's that you're looking at?"

She put the sheet of paper onto her desk. It was a picture of the photo frame I'd decorated. On the picture, someone had written, 'Jill Maxwell made this monstrosity.'

"Where did you get that from, Mrs V?"

"It was on my desk when I arrived this morning. I assumed you'd left it there. I'm sorry to have to say this, Jill. I thought what you'd done to the desk was bad, but this is much worse. I'm not even sure what it's supposed to be." She squinted again at the picture. "Is it some kind of photo frame?"

"I've never seen it before in my life." I took the sheet of paper from her and screwed it into a ball. "It must be someone's idea of a practical joke. Excuse me, would you?"

Livid, I charged into my office where Winky was busy broadcasting.

"Winky FM brings you this week's record of the week, Cat Boy and The Nips."

I hurried behind the screen and yanked off his headphones.

"Hey, do you mind?" He looked suitably outraged. "You could have had my ears off."

"Never mind your ears." I straightened out the crumpled piece of paper. "Would you care to explain this?"

"I think it's you who owes the world an explanation. What is that thing meant to be?"

"How did you get hold of this picture?"

"I have my methods."

"Why did you put it on Mrs V's desk?"

"It's such a perfect piece of art that I wanted to share it with the world. That's why I put it on Instagram too."

"You've done what?"

"And the last time I looked, it already had thirty-five comments. You should read them. They're hilarious."

An hour later, I was still seething over what Winky had done. Sooner or later, though, I'd get my own back. You see if I don't. Meanwhile, he was back behind the screen, doing his DJ thing.

So far, I'd made little or no progress on the Edward Broom case, so I decided to check The Bugle's archives around the date of his disappearance. The headline story for the day he'd been scheduled to check out was about an altercation at the Lakeside Tavern. The following day's lead story was about a cat that had got trapped on the fire station roof. Next up was a story about a woman who had found a thirty-year old packet of biscuits under her grandmother's bed. It had clearly been a slow news week. Nowhere, though, could I find any mention of Broom's disappearance.

After that abysmal failure, I decided to take a different approach. This time, I accessed a database of all the major newspapers in a fifty-mile radius, using the search terms: hotel and disappearance.

It was only when the results appeared on screen that I realised I'd failed to specify an end date, so there were entries dated up to the current day – the most recent of which was the case that Jack was working on.

There was only one item related to Edward Broom. The short article, which was dated a couple of weeks after he'd vanished, said little more than that a man had disappeared from Parkside Hotel. One thing that did surprise me, though, was the number of people who had gone missing from hotels during the last two years.

I was getting nowhere fast, so I decided to make another attempt to talk to Eddie Broom's wife, Sandra. I'd already called her several times, and she'd made it crystal clear that she didn't want to speak to me. This time, though, I planned to turn up on her doorstep, on the basis that it was far more difficult to turn someone away when they were right there in front of you.

"I'm nipping out for a while, Mrs V."

"Okay, dear. By the way, did you remember to ask Jack about dinner?"

Oh, bum! There was no way I could tell her that I'd forgotten a third time.

"Of course, I did. He suggested next Wednesday, if that works for you."

"That will be fine. Is seven o'clock okay?"

"Perfect."

"I'm really looking forward to having you both over."

"Me too."

I needed something to fortify me ahead of my confrontation with Sandra Broom, and I knew just the thing. Next stop, Coffee Games.

"Can I get a caramel latte and a blueberry muffin, please?"

Piers stared at me but didn't move.

"Piers, did you hear me? I'd like a caramel latte and a blueberry muffin, please."

Still he didn't react.

I was getting really annoyed now.

"Piers, whatever's the matter?"

He gestured to a sign on the wall at the side of the counter that read:

Today's game: Simon Says

Now everything made sense, so I tried again, "Simon says, will you get me a caramel latte and a blueberry muffin please, Piers."

"Certainly Jill, coming straight up."

Once I had my drink and cake, I took a seat at a table near the window. No sooner had I sat down, than Betty Longbottom came to join me. She was dressed to the nines and had obviously spent the last half hour in makeup.

"Good morning, Jill," she said in her fake posh voice.

"Morning, Betty."

"We high-flying businesswomen need our coffee breaks, don't we, Jill?"

"Err? Yeah, I guess so." Why was she acting all weird again? "Look, Betty, I'm really sorry about the pigeon incident the other day."

"Let's not talk about that," she snapped.

"But it must have been embarrassing for you when that pigeon landed on my shoulder. It's not really the image you were trying to portray."

She turned around and shouted over her shoulder, "Cut! Cut! I don't want any of that included in the show."

Only then did I realise there was a camera crew hovering in the background.

"Really, Jill," she said in her normal voice. "I'm trying to create a good impression here. The least you could do is to play along."

"I would have done if I'd realised you were on-camera."

"The next time I see you, if I speak in a posh voice, it means the camera crew is filming me, and you need to be on your best behaviour. Okay?"

"Okay, Betty, whatever you say."

Sheesh!

I was on my way back up the high street when I spotted Armi, a few yards in front of me. I was about to call to him when he ducked inside Ever. I couldn't for the life of me think why he'd have occasion to go in there.

Curiosity got the better of me and I followed him inside. As I walked through the door, I spotted him on the stairs, headed for the roof terrace, so I did the same. There was no one else up there, so I held back and watched what he did. He headed to a small apple tree, which certainly hadn't been there on my previous visit. Armi then took what appeared to be a twenty-pound note out of his pocket and placed it in the box next to the tree. Next, he picked an apple, and shoved it in his pocket.

As he made his way back to the stairs, I stepped out in front of him.

"Armi, what are you doing up here?"

"Nothing." He couldn't have looked any more guilty if he'd tried.

"I saw you put money in that box and then take an apple."

"You won't tell Annabel about any of this will you?"

"Tell her what?"

"I heard about it from a friend of a friend."

"Heard about what, Armi? You aren't making any sense."

"I was told that the apples on that tree are supposed to make you feel twenty years younger. I didn't believe it at first, but I decided it couldn't do any harm to give it a try. To my amazement, it actually worked. The results are remarkable. I feel just like a young man again."

That explained why Armi had been feeling so frisky recently.

"I see."

"You won't say anything, will you, Jill?"

"Of course not. Your secret is safe with me."

"Thanks. I'd better get going." He shot off down the stairs.

I was intrigued to find out more about the so-called magical apples, so I walked over to the tree. What Armi had told me was clearly nonsense, but I was still tempted to try one, just to see what happened.

I was about to pick an apple when —

"Leave those apples alone or put twenty pounds in the box."

It was Grandma's voice, but I had no idea where it was coming from. There was no sign of cameras, so how did she know I was about to take an apple?

I hurried downstairs to her office, knocked twice, and went inside. Thankfully, Grandma was wearing shoes today.

"Well, look who it is. Two visits from my granddaughter in the same week. To what do I owe this honour?"

"How did you know I was about to take one of those apples?"

"You should know by now. I'm all seeing and all hearing."

"What's the story with the apples? I just saw Armi up there and he seems to think that they can make you feel twenty years younger."

"That's because they do."

"That's nonsense, and you know it. I hope you're not poisoning them with some kind of weird potion."

"Relax. I'm not poisoning anyone. It's just an illusion potion that makes them think they feel twenty years younger. It doesn't actually have any effect on them at all."

"I might've known. I suppose you're making a small fortune from this."

"Obviously. Humans are such easy targets; it would be remiss of me not to take advantage of them."

"Unbelievable."

"I hope you're ready for Saturday's broom flying practice."

"As ready as I'll ever be."

***

Lorraine Cross had told me that her brother's widow, Sandra, had moved to a larger house, shortly after Eddie had disappeared. Judging by her new house, and the car parked in the driveway, Sandra Broom certainly wasn't short of money.

I wasn't anticipating a particularly warm welcome, so I took a deep breath, braced myself, and then knocked on the door.

The woman who answered it looked as though she was dressed for a cocktail party. She was wearing designer clothes and her jewellery was probably worth more than my house.

"Can I help you?" She looked me up and down as though I was something nasty that she'd just trodden in.

"My name is Jill Maxwell. I wondered if you could spare me a few minutes?"

"Are you the woman who keeps phoning me? That private investigator woman?"

"That's me."

"I thought I made myself quite clear; I have nothing to say to you. I'd like you to leave now, please."

"I'm sorry, Mrs Broom, but I can't do that."

"If you don't, I'll call the police."

"If you must, you must, but I'm not moving from this spot. Wouldn't it be easier to spare me five minutes of your time? And then you'll never see me again."

"All right." She sighed. "You'd better come in. But five minutes and not a moment longer."

She led the way into an elaborately furnished dining room, where she sat at the head of the table. She didn't offer me a seat.

"What exactly is it you want?"

"Just to ask a few questions about Eddie."

"It's Edward!"

"Sorry. Your husband's sister has asked me to investigate his disappearance. It's been over two years now."

"I don't need you to remind me how long it's been. I'm perfectly well aware, thank you very much."

"If you don't mind me saying so, Mrs Broom, I can't understand why you'd object to my investigation. Surely you want to know what happened to Edward?"

"Frankly, dear, I don't care. I gave up on that man a long time ago. Did you know he was having an affair?"

"No, I didn't."

"I didn't think so. That sister of his thinks Edward is some kind of saint, but he's anything but that."

"Do you think it's possible he ran away with his mistress?"

"When he disappeared, that was the first thought that crossed my mind, but then that brazen hussy came to see me a couple of weeks after he'd gone missing, to ask if I knew where he was. Can you imagine? The sheer audacity of the woman."

"Did she seem genuine or could it have been some kind of act?"

"She seemed genuine enough."

"What did you say to her?"

"I'm afraid that isn't repeatable."

"Would you mind giving me the woman's name?"

"Sylvia Long. She and Edward worked together."

"Do you know how long the affair had been going on?"

"I neither know nor care. I found out about it a couple of months before Edward disappeared." She checked her watch. "You've had your five minutes now. I'd like you to leave."

Chapter 10

I hadn't seen that one coming. Why hadn't Lorraine Cross mentioned that her brother was having an affair? Was it possible that she didn't know? Or had she decided to withhold that information for some reason? Was Sylvia Long the mysterious woman who Denise Black had seen with Edward Broom? Had he deliberately 'vanished' so that he could be with his mistress? If so, why had she turned up at Sandra Broom's house, supposedly looking for him?

None of this made a lick of sense.

I needed to speak to Sylvia Long, so I made a phone call to Branded Context, only to discover that she'd left the company a year earlier. I asked if they'd give me her forwarding address or phone number, but they refused.

***

When I entered my office building there were two clowns staring down at me from the landing. It was only when I was halfway up the stairs that I realised it was actually a large sign, featuring life-size clowns. They were holding an arrow pointing down the corridor to Jimmy and Kimmy's school.

"I suppose you've seen it, Mrs V."

"The clown sign? Yes, I have."

"I know that I asked Jimmy and Kimmy to put up a new sign at the top of the stairs, but it never for one minute occurred to me that they'd come up with that monstrosity. It's even worse than the original sign. What will people think when they come through the door and see a couple of clowns looking down at them? They'll run a mile."

"A lot of people like clowns, Jill."

"Don't be ridiculous."

"What are you going to do about it?"

"I don't know. I should wait a while because if I go down there now, I'll probably fall out with someone. Mrs V, would you see if you can trace a woman called Sylvia Long who used to work at a company called Branded Context?"

"Is that all the information you have on her?"

"I'm afraid so."

"It isn't much to go on."

"Just do your best, would you?"

Much to my surprise, Winky wasn't broadcasting. In fact, there was no sign of him, which was just as well, because I still hadn't forgiven him for what he'd done with the picture of my photo frame. The last time I'd checked, there were two-hundred and thirty-four comments on Instagram, and none of them were complimentary.

I was busy shuffling paperwork when Mrs V popped her head around the door.

"Jill, I've got two gentlemen out here to see you."

"I'm not expecting anyone, am I?"

"No, they say they're from Ofcom."

"Off what?"

"Ofcom. They insist on speaking to whoever is in charge."

"I suppose that's me. You'd better send them in."

The two men were dressed in identical drab suits. The tallest of the two was wearing a hat; the smaller one was bald.

"Hello, gentlemen. How can I help you today?"

"Are you in charge here?" the taller of the two said.

"Yes, I am. My name's Jill Maxwell."

"In that case, Ms Maxwell, perhaps you'd be kind enough to explain why you are broadcasting from these premises without a licence."

Oh bum! I was going to kill Winky.

"I'm sorry, gentlemen, but I have no idea what you're talking about. I'm a private investigator and this is my office."

"Are you trying to tell us that you aren't running a radio station from here?"

"A radio station?" I laughed. "Of course not. Whatever gave you that idea?"

"You deny it, then?"

"Of course I do. The idea is preposterous."

"In that case, you won't mind if we take a look around, will you?"

"I'm sorry, but I can't allow you to do that. I'm very busy at the moment."

"I'm afraid you don't have any choice in the matter." He took out some paperwork and placed it on my desk. "This grants us permission to search your premises."

Before I could stop him, the smaller man walked across the office and pulled back the screen.

"What do we have here?" He smirked.

"How did that get there?" I did my best to sound suitably surprised.

"This looks remarkably like a radio studio to me, Ms Maxwell," the guy with the hat said.

"Oh yes, of course. Silly me. I'd totally forgotten that

was there. It must have been left by the previous occupant."

"My understanding was that you've occupied these same premises for several years."

"That's true, and I've been meaning to get rid of that junk ever since."

"In that case, perhaps you'd care to tell us who has been broadcasting a station called Winky FM from these premises for the last few days. We have recordings, if you'd care to hear them?"

"That won't be necessary."

"So, who was it?"

"You wouldn't believe me if I told you."

"Try me."

***

Madge Rumbelow clearly missed her daughter, Cynthia, and she desperately wanted to make contact with her. Unfortunately, Cynthia was a non-believer and would have no truck with the afterlife.

I hadn't said anything to Madge because I didn't want to get her hopes up, but I was going to try to persuade Cynthia to be more open-minded about the spirit world. That wasn't going to be easy because she didn't know me from Adam, and she was unlikely to be receptive to a stranger who turned up on her doorstep and told her that she ought to believe in ghosts.

Still, nothing ventured, nothing gained.

On my way to the car, who should I bump into but Luther, with a pretty young woman on his arm. I assumed it must be his new girlfriend, Rebecca, who had not only lifted his spirits, but had also got him in the best shape of his life. As I drew closer, I realised that she was a werewolf; a very pretty werewolf.

"Hi, Jill, fancy meeting you here," Luther said. "I hope my report didn't upset you too much."

"Of course not. It was pretty much what I expected."

"This is Rebecca. I think I may have mentioned her to you the other day."

"Only about a thousand times." I turned to her. "He never stopped talking about you. It's nice to meet you."

She blushed. "You too."

"I was only saying to Rebecca last night that we should have dinner with you and Jack some time," Luther said. "In fact, I was going to phone you later today, to try to arrange something, but seeing as we've bumped into one another, maybe we could do it now?"

"We'd love that, but the thing is, our social calendar is chock-a-block for the next few days. We could make it a week tomorrow if that works for you?"

"That would be great, wouldn't it, Rebecca?" She nodded. Somewhat less enthusiastically, I thought. Oblivious to her reaction, Luther continued. "Great, next Friday it is, then. I'll give you a call beforehand to arrange the details."

***

Madge Rumbelow's daughter, Cynthia, had her mother's eyes and mouth. Unfortunately for me, what came out of her mouth wasn't exactly encouraging.

"Let me get this straight," she snapped. "You turn up

on my doorstep and expect me to believe that my mother's ghost has been in touch with you. Have I got that right?"

"Yeah, pretty much."

"Do I look like I've just fallen off the top of a Christmas tree? I don't know how people like you have the nerve to do this type of thing. Do you have no conscience at all?"

"I'm really sorry you feel that way, but I promise it's the truth. I'm a medium not a conman. I didn't choose to be contacted by your mother. It just happened. I have absolutely nothing to gain by telling you this."

"Yeah, right. You're just as bad as the other guy who came here."

"What other guy?"

"The guy who was running the same kind of scam as you are. I suppose you have some of my mother's jewellery that you'd like to sell to me too?"

"I'm sorry, but you have me totally confused now. What jewellery?"

"The guy gave me a photograph of the jewellery that he claimed had belonged to my mother. I'm going to tell you what I told him. You're a liar and a con artist, and I'm not buying your jewellery."

"I honestly don't know anything about this man, and I don't have any jewellery to sell. The only thing I wanted to do was to let you know that your mother would like to get in touch with you."

"And now you've told me, so you can do one."

"Before I go, can I ask a favour?"

"You've got a nerve." She laughed. "I'll give you that."

"Do you still have the photograph of the jewellery that the man gave you?"

"Yes. Why?"

"Could I have it?"

"If I give it to you, will you sling your hook?"

"Yes, I promise."

"Wait there." She went back into the house and returned a few minutes later. "Here, take it, and I never want to see you again."

"Thanks." I flipped the photograph over. "What's this number on the back?"

"It's the guy's phone number. He told me to call him if I changed my mind about buying the jewellery. As if. Now please leave and never come back."

"Thank—" The door had already been slammed in my face.

I hadn't got the result I'd hoped for—Cynthia was still an unbeliever as far as the afterlife was concerned, but I hadn't come away empty-handed because the jewellery in the photo looked remarkably like that which Madge had described to me.

***

I should have done a big shop a couple of days ago, but I'd never got around to it, so I called at the corner shop on my way home.

Little Jack had a new pair of stilts.

"They're very colourful, Jack."

He clearly couldn't hear what I was saying, so I pressed the button on the intercom.

"Your new stilts are very colourful."

"Do you like them? The other ones were rather boring, I thought."

"The light blue is much better."

"Turquoise, actually."

Whatever. "Are the hand-held scanners working yet?"

"Yes, they're fine now."

By the time I'd got everything I needed, my basket was full, and I'd scanned every item. Back at the counter, I pressed the intercom and said, "Jack, do I press the green buy button now?"

"Yes please, Jill. That's all you need do."

After I'd done that, he checked his screen and said, "That'll be twenty-two pence, please."

I stared at the basket full of goods, which by a conservative estimate should have cost at least thirty pounds. Then I handed him fifty-pence and told him to keep the change.

What? Of course I'm joking. Obviously, I told him that the scanner still wasn't working properly. Sheesh, what do you take me for?

***

Jack and I had just finished dinner.

"Do you have your diary handy, Jack?"

"I don't have a diary. You know I don't have a diary. I've never had one."

"You'd better get one because our social life has just taken off."

"How come?"

"You're going bowling with Peter while I get together with Kathy and Martin next Tuesday. Right?"

"Yeah?"

"Then, on Wednesday, you and I have been invited to

dinner at Mrs V's house."

"That's great. I'm really looking forward to seeing her new place."

"That's not all. On Friday we're having dinner with Luther and his new girlfriend, Rebecca."

"Fantastic. I'm all in favour of dining out. It saves me the trouble of having to cook."

"What do you mean it saves *you* the trouble? We take turns."

"And when was the last time you cooked?"

"It must have been yesterday."

"I don't think so."

"The day before, then."

"Think again."

"Anyway, I thought I'd better warn you that Rebecca is a werewolf."

"Does Luther know?"

"Yes, he knows." I rolled my eyes. "Of course he doesn't know."

"Is it safe for him to go out with a werewolf?"

"Perfectly safe unless she decides to turn, and I'm sure she's too sensible to do that. She seems really nice, but a little shy."

After we'd finished dinner, we went through to the lounge.

"Have you made any progress with that cold case you're working on?" Jack asked.

"No. I'm getting nowhere fast. All I know so far is the guy was seen by the housekeeper twice on the day he checked in, but that's the last anyone saw of him."

"That's pretty much what happened with the case I'm

working on at the moment. The guy was seen on the day he checked in, but never again."

"Freaky."

Chapter 11

The next morning, Jack had already left for work. As I had a little time before I needed to leave the house, I thought I'd sort through my bag, which was full of rubbish. Near to the bottom, I found the small trinket box that Edith Petalwhite, the fairy godmother, had given to me. It was just as ugly as I remembered, and I was curious to see if there was anything inside. It didn't rattle, but maybe that was because it was chock-full of priceless jewellery.

I can dream, can't I?

Edith hadn't had a key for it, but the lock didn't look very substantial so I figured I could probably force it open. Using a small screwdriver from the kitchen drawer, I started fiddling around with the lock. After a couple of minutes, there was a click and the lid sprang open. The room was immediately filled with a light green smoke, which almost choked me. When it had eventually cleared and I could see again, there was a giant green man standing in the kitchen. He was so tall that he had to bend double in order not to bang his head on the ceiling.

"Where am I?" The man looked a little disorientated.

"Hi." I gave him a little wave. "Did you just come out of that trinket box?"

"Yes, and I have terrible leg cramp."

"Are you a genie?"

"Do I look like Jeanie? My name is Alexander Biggins, but everybody calls me Big."

"Have you been in that box for a long time?"

"That depends on what you consider to be a long time. A few hundred years, give or take."

"Wasn't it claustrophobic in there?"

"I didn't really notice. I was asleep most of the time."

"Now that I've released you, do I get three wishes?"

"How am I supposed to give you wishes?"

"I thought that's what genies did."

"Why do you insist on calling me Jeanie? I've already told you my name is Big."

"Sorry, but if you can't grant me any wishes, I might as well go to work." I grabbed my bag. "You'd better get back inside your box."

"And how am I supposed to get into that little thing? Look at the size of me."

"But you just came out of it. How did you get in there before?"

"I don't know. Someone put me in there, I guess. Can you put me back in?"

"I can give it a go." I tried to cast the 'shrink' spell on him, but it had no effect. "I'm sorry, Big, I don't know what else to do, and I really do have to go to work."

"That's okay. I'll come with you."

"You can't. What will people say?"

"No one can see me apart from you."

"Even so, you'll still have to stay here."

"I can't. The rules say that I have to stay by the side of whoever releases me from the box."

"But you'll never get into the car."

Despite my protestations, Big insisted on getting into the car with me. He somehow managed to squeeze into the back seat, but he was so large that his legs spilled over into the front. There was barely enough room for me to get into the driver's seat, so I ended up squashed against the window.

I was just about to set off when someone tapped on the window at the side of me; it was Clare from next-door.

"Are you okay, Jill?"

I lowered the window. "Yes, thank you."

"I only ask because you seem to be sitting in a rather peculiar position."

"I've tweaked my back and I find it easier to drive if I sit to one side, like this."

"I see. Are you sure you're okay to drive?"

"Absolutely, but thanks for asking. I have to get going because I'm running late."

Mr Ivers was looking every bit as unhappy as the last time I'd seen him. He barely acknowledged me, other than to hold out his hand for my payment. It was only then that I realised that my bag was on the passenger seat underneath Big's legs.

"Mr Ivers, I'm very sorry, but I seem to have come out without my bag."

"Oh dear, that is unfortunate. Don't worry, though, because you can turn the car around over there, and go back to your house for it."

"I was just wondering. Do you think you could possibly allow me to go through the barrier? I could pay you double when I come home tonight."

"I'd love to, Jill, but I'm afraid that's against the rules."

"Okay. How about if you were to lend me the money until tonight?"

"That too is against the rules, unfortunately. I'm most terribly sorry."

He didn't look sorry. In fact, he actually looked happier than he had two minutes earlier.

"Thanks for nothing." I made a three-point turn, but I didn't drive all the way home. Instead, I parked in the layby just down the road.

"Big, you'll have to lift up your legs so I can get to my bag."

"I can't move them."

"You're going to have to try, okay?"

"Can you see it now?"

"You need to lift them a little higher."

"How about now?"

"That's it."

I grabbed my bag, fished out some change, did another three-point turn, and then headed back to the toll bridge.

"That was quick, Jill." Mr Ivers looked surprised to see me again so soon. "I hope you weren't speeding."

"Of course not. I realised that my bag was in the boot. Here's your money."

***

After I'd parked the car, it took Big almost five minutes to extract himself from the backseat. He only managed it then with a little help from me. I grabbed one of his arms and pulled. He didn't move at first, but eventually, after a lot of effort, he popped out like a cork from a bottle, which sent me tumbling backwards onto my bottom. A woman who was walking by spotted me on the floor, shook her head and tutted loudly. She clearly thought I was drunk.

As we walked to the office building, I was very conscious of the fact that I had a giant green man at my side. And, even though I was the only person who could see him, it still felt really weird. Big seemed totally unaware of just how tall he was, with the result that he banged his head on the door as we entered the office building.

After we'd climbed the stairs and were approaching the outer office, I said, "Bend down. Watch your head!"

Mrs V gave me a puzzled look. "Who were you talking to, Jill?"

"Err—there was a very tall guy following me up the stairs. I thought he was coming in here, but he must have gone down the corridor to the clown school."

"I see. You'll be pleased to know that I managed to find the address for Sylvia Long."

"That's excellent work, Mrs V."

"Thank you. I've put the information on your desk."

As we went through to my office, Big once again failed to bend low enough, and he banged his head on the door frame.

"Ouch." He rubbed his forehead. "Why are all these doors so tiny?"

"It's not the door that's tiny, it's you who's too tall."

Winky, who was sitting on the sofa, gave me a puzzled look. "Who are you talking to?"

"To Big." I pointed towards the door.

"Big what?"

"That's his name."

"And is Big your imaginary friend?"

"No, he isn't. I know you can't see him, but he's standing right over there. He's a very tall, green man."

"I knew this day would come sooner or later." Winky shook his head. "It was only a matter of time. Still, we've had a good run, you and I."

"What are you talking about?"

"You've clearly lost the plot completely this time. I expect the men in white coats to be here at any moment."

"I have not lost the plot. He really is standing there. His name is Alexander Biggins, or Big for short."

"*Big* for *short*?" Winky laughed. "That's very good."

"A fairy godmother gave me a trinket box, and when I opened it, Big popped out."

"I can't wait to hear you telling this to the men in white coats."

"It's true. The problem is that neither of us knows how to get him back into the trinket box, and until we can find a way to do that, he has to stay with me."

"If you say so."

"Anyway, Winky, I have a bone to pick with you."

"What have I done now?"

"I had a visit yesterday from Ofcom."

"Off who?"

"The people who license broadcasters."

"Oh, them."

"Yes, them. They wanted to know why I was broadcasting out of this office."

"What did you tell them?"

"I managed to persuade them that my young nephew had been playing around with the equipment, but that I had no idea he was actually on the air. They made me promise that there'd be no more broadcasts, and that I'd get rid of the equipment by next Monday."

"You can't do that. What about Winky FM?"

"I don't give two hoots about Winky FM. If you want to continue with it, you'll have to find somewhere else to do it because if this equipment hasn't been moved by next

Monday, it's going to the tip, and you'll be a dead cat."

***

I wanted to find out why Lorraine Cross had failed to tell me that her brother was having an affair, so I gave her a call.

"Jill? Have you got some news for me already?"

"I'm afraid not. It is still early days, though."

"Sorry, I'm just so desperate to know what's happened to Eddie."

"I understand. The reason I called is to ask if you know a woman called Sylvia Long."

The silence on the other end of the phone answered my question, but eventually Lorraine said, "You found out about her, then?"

"Yes, but it would have been far better if you'd told me in the first place. Why didn't you?"

"I'm really sorry, Jill. I should have, but I thought if I did, you'd jump to the conclusion that Eddie had run off with Sylvia. Just like everyone else seems to have done."

"Surely you must realise that's a possibility."

"I don't think so. He only started seeing Sylvia because he was so unhappy with Sandra. Have you spoken to Sandra yet?"

"Yes, she was the one who told me about Sylvia."

"In that case, you'll know what a nasty piece of work Sandra is. I couldn't blame him for looking for happiness elsewhere."

"Is there anything else that you haven't told me? Because if there is, now would be the time to do so."

"No, I promise. You know everything there is to know

now. I'm really sorry I didn't tell you about Sylvia before."

"Okay. I'll keep you posted."

Over in the corner, Big yawned and stretched. "I'm bored."

"What do you mean, you're bored?"

"There's nothing to do in here."

"You were stuck inside a little box for hundreds of years, and you weren't bored then. How can you be now?"

"I slept most of the time when I was in the trinket box, but I can't get to sleep here with all the noise that you and that cat are making."

"I'm very sorry about that, but you'll just have to put up with it until such time as I can find a way to get you back into the box."

I glanced over at Winky who was staring at me, incredulously.

"What?" I snapped.

"Nothing." He shrugged. "I'm just sitting here minding my own business, listening to you talking to the wall."

***

When I contacted Sylvia Long, I expected a hostile reception, but she seemed keen to speak to me, and said I could pop over to see her that same afternoon.

Although that was great news, the last thing I needed was a long journey stuck in the car with a big green man. Fortunately, I'd come up with a fantastic plan.

I'd found Washbridge Trailer Rental in the Yellow

Pages.

"Yes, madam," said the eager shop assistant. "How can I help?"

"Hi, I need to rent a trailer for a short period of time."

"In that case, you've come to the right place. We have trailers of all shapes and sizes, and you can hire them for short or long periods. Perhaps you could start by telling me what it is you want to transport."

I glanced at Big, who was standing right next to me. "It's a big thing."

"A big *thing*? Right. How big, exactly?"

"About twelve-foot tall."

"What about the other dimensions?"

"Not too fat."

"*Fat?*"

"I meant wide. Not too wide."

"I'm afraid I'm going to need a bit more than that, madam."

"Think of a telephone box. A very tall telephone box."

"And how heavy is this *tall telephone box*?"

"Quite heavy, I would say."

"In that case, I think you're going to need the CarryAll 673. If you'd like to follow me, I'll show you the model I have in mind."

He led the way into the showroom where there were several rows of trailers on display.

"This is the one. Do you think this will be okay for your needs?"

"I think so." I turned to Big and gestured for him to get into the trailer, but he clearly had no idea what I was trying to tell him, so I said, in a hushed voice, "Get in there."

"I'm sorry, madam," the sales assistant said. "I'm not allowed to do that."

"No, of course not. Sorry."

Fortunately, Big had now realised what I wanted him to do, and he climbed into the trailer.

"Yes, this one is just the ticket," I said. "How much does it cost?"

"How long will you need it for?"

"I'm not really sure."

"It's thirty pounds a day or one-hundred and ninety pounds for the week."

"Can I just pay a deposit for now and pay the balance when I bring it back?"

"Of course, madam. That will be fine."

Chapter 12

I'd spent the last ten minutes trying to persuade Big to let me strap him into the trailer, but he'd refused point blank; he insisted that he'd be perfectly safe just holding onto the sides. In the end, I had no option but to allow him to do as he pleased.

About half a mile down the road. I checked my rear-view mirror, only to find that the trailer was empty. I quickly pulled into the side of the road, got out of the car, and started to walk back the way I'd come. I'd not gone very far when I saw a large green figure in the distance hobbling towards me.

"Are you okay, Big?"

"I'm fine." He looked a little shaky and was dusting himself down.

"Are you sure? You must have fallen with a bang."

"I've told you, I'm fine."

"Are you going to allow me to strap you in the trailer now?"

"Yes, okay."

***

Sylvia Long, an attractive woman in her mid-forties, lived in an upmarket apartment on the outskirts of Wakefield.

Our discussion was not an easy one. Not because Sylvia was in anyway obstructive, but because I found it hard to concentrate with a tall green man sitting in the corner of her lounge. What made it worse was that ten minutes into the interview, Big decided to start picking his nose.

Despite those distractions I did the best I could.

"Have you actually met Eddie's sister, Lorraine?" I said.

"No, but he often spoke of her. I got the impression that the two of them were very close."

"I went to see his wife yesterday."

"Sandra? I don't suppose that horrible cow cares whether you find Eddie or not, does she?"

"I think it's fair to say she wasn't as distraught as I would have expected her to be. From what I could make out, she thought he'd run away with you. At least she did until you turned up on her doorstep to ask if she knew where he was."

Sylvia managed a smile. "I'm not sure how I found the courage to do that, but I was so desperate for information. Any information."

"How serious was your relationship with Eddie?"

"Very. For me at least. I loved him from the moment we first met."

"What about him? Did he feel the same way?"

"I'm not sure anymore. I thought he loved me, but now —" Her words drifted away.

"Had the two of you ever discussed the possibility of him leaving Sandra?"

"Often."

"With what result?"

"He said he was going to do it, but that he needed more time."

Hmm. A likely story.

"What about the day he disappeared? Were you at the hotel with him?"

"Yes. The room was booked in his name, just in case Sandra checked up on him."

"Can you tell me exactly what happened while you were there?"

"There's not much to tell really. We'd spent a lovely day together and then, in the evening, we went out for a meal."

"You didn't eat at the hotel?"

"No, we checked the menu, but there was nothing on there that we fancied, so we went to the Lakeside Tavern. The meal was lovely, and everything was going great until I made the mistake of asking him again when he was going to leave Sandra. "He told me that I should drop the subject, and not to spoil the evening. I should have let it go. I see that now. But I'd had a couple of drinks, and I was fed up of being fobbed off, so I accused him of stalling. I told him that I didn't think he was ever going to leave her, and then I stormed out. That was the last time I ever saw or heard from him."

On the drive back to Washbridge, I mulled over what Sylvia had told me. Eddie Broom's marriage had clearly been on the rocks, and then his mistress had walked out on him. Had that been the straw that had broken the camel's back? Was it possible he'd decided he couldn't take any more and chosen to 'vanish'?

Or had something more sinister taken place?

***

Back at the office, I decided it was time to tackle the sign problem, so I took a walk down the corridor to the offices of Clown.

"Where are we going now?" Big said.

"I have to have a word with a couple of clowns."

"Great! I love clowns."

"Don't be ridiculous."

Kimmy was on reception as usual.

"We got rid of that sign like you asked, Jill."

"So I noticed, Kimmy."

"It's actually Sneezy when I'm on duty. Did you also notice that we'd put up a new one at the top of the stairs like you suggested?"

"Yes, *Sneezy*, I did, but then, I could hardly miss it."

"Do you like it?"

"No, I don't. When I suggested a sign at the top of the stairs, I had in mind something a little more subtle. A small plain sign that said, 'Clown school this way.' What I wasn't expecting was a ginormous sign featuring two life-size clowns."

"We rather like them."

"I'm sure you do, but surely you must see my problem. When a new client comes to visit me, the first thing they'll see when they walk in the building is two clowns staring down at them. What kind of impression do you think that will give them?"

"Everyone likes clowns, Jill."

"I love them," Big chimed in.

"Shut up, you. I didn't ask for your opinion."

"There was no call for that, Jill." Kimmy looked positively taken aback.

"No, not you. Sorry, what I meant to say is not everyone likes clowns. I don't for starters."

"You're just saying that."

"I'm really not. And I'm not the only person who

doesn't like them. You're going to have to get that new sign replaced."

"I don't know what Breezy will have to say about that. He wasn't very happy when I told him that we had to get the first one replaced."

"In that case, he and I had better have a little chat."

"He's not in today, but I can ask him to come and see you on Monday."

"I look forward to it."

"You were a bit hard on her," Big said, as we walked back down the corridor.

"What did I just say about not asking for your opinion? Watch your head on the door."

"I've spoken to those clowns about their sign, Mrs V."

"What did they say?"

"Jimmy or Breezy or whatever he calls himself is coming to see me on Monday. We're going to have a friendly chat."

"You'll be gentle with him, won't you?"

"You know me, Mrs V."

"That's the problem. I do."

When I walked into my office, I couldn't believe my ears: Winky was broadcasting again.

"This is Winky FM on air for the last time."

I hurried across the room, pulled back the screen, and yanked off his headphones.

"Hey, what are you doing?" he screamed at me.

"What did I tell you? No more broadcasting."

"I'm just saying goodbye to my listeners."

I picked up the microphone, walked over to the

window, and threw it out.

"Hey, you can't do that."

"I just did."

"That microphone was expensive."

"I don't care. I warned you that I could get arrested if you made any more broadcasts from here. Get rid of the rest of this stuff, and do it now."

When I turned around, Big was cowering in the corner.

"What's up with you?"

"You're scary when you're angry," he said.

"This is nothing. You should see me when I—"

"Turn green?"

"What? No. When I'm really vexed. Now, you two had better stay quiet for a while because I have work to do."

"Two?" Winky gave me a look, but he had the good sense not to pass further comment.

A few minutes later, I heard voices coming from the outer office. Being curious by nature (okay, nosey), I went to find out who was out there.

Mrs V was talking to Jules who was sitting in Mrs V's chair. The young woman looked quite pale.

"Hi, Jules, are you okay?"

"She's just had a nasty shock," Mrs V said.

"Oh dear, what happened?"

"I'm okay, Jill. As I was on my way here, a microphone hit the ground right in front of me. I think someone must have thrown it out of one of the windows."

Oh bum!

"Are you sure you're okay?"

"Positive. It just shook me up a little. Why would someone do something like that?"

"I can't imagine. Unless of course their patience had been tested to the limit."

Both Jules and Mrs V gave me the same puzzled look.

"Not that that would be any excuse, obviously. Would you like a drink? Tea maybe?"

"No, thanks. I only popped in to ask if you and Annabel would sponsor me in the Washbridge Marathon tomorrow."

"Of course we will," Mrs V said. "Won't we, Jill?"

"Actually, I've already sponsored our next-door neighbours."

"But you'll want to sponsor Jules as well, won't you?" Mrs V said.

"Will I? I mean, yes, of course I will."

"That's great." Jules took a form out of her bag and handed it to Mrs V.

"Is ten-pence a mile all right, Jules?" Mrs V said.

"That's far too much, Annabel. Make it five-pence a mile. That's more than enough."

After Mrs V had filled in the form, she turned to me and said, "How much shall I put you down for, Jill? The same?"

"Err, yeah, I guess so." I took a closer look at the form. "How come you and Dexter didn't go for one of those joint sponsorship forms?"

"We thought it would be better to have separate ones. And besides, I think those joint ones are a bit of a con. People have no idea what they're committing to."

"How do you mean?"

"If you tick the checkbox, and both runners finish in under three hours, the amount you agreed to sponsor is multiplied by ten. That just doesn't sit right with me."

It didn't sit right with me either. I couldn't believe Britt's nerve. When Jack had asked her about the checkbox, she'd glossed over it as though it was nothing. If the Livelys both finished inside of three hours, it was going to cost us a small fortune.

Unless of course I did something about it.

Tee-hee.

Big had been sitting in the corner of my office for the last hour and a half, and for the last ten minutes, he'd done nothing but complain.

"How much longer do we have to stay here? It's boring."

I checked my watch. It was just after four-thirty, so I decided I might as well call it a day.

"We can go home now."

"Great!" He stood up and banged his head on the ceiling.

"Be careful."

As I walked out of the door, Winky caught my eye, and said, "Are you sure you don't need a medical intervention?"

"You'll need it if you do any more broadcasting."

"I'm going to call it a day, Mrs V."

"Okay, Jill. I'll see you in the morning."

It had been one of those days when I felt like I'd achieved very little, but then the drive to Wakefield and back to see Sylvia Long had taken several hours out of my day.

When we got to the car, Big climbed into the trailer. This time, though, he didn't need any persuading to let me strap him in. At the toll bridge, I took out the usual change from my bag and handed it to Mr Ivers.

"I need another twenty-five pence, please, Jill."

"Sorry?"

"Another twenty-five pence, please."

"Have the charges gone up again?"

"No. The additional charge is for your trailer."

"Surely you don't charge for those."

"Yes, we do." He pointed to the sign.

I'd never really taken much notice of the list of charges before because I'd always paid the same fee.

"Great." I took another twenty-five pence out of my purse and handed it to him.

When I arrived home, Jack's car was already on the driveway. As I unstrapped Big from the trailer, I said to him, "You have to be on your best behaviour in here."

"I will, but is there anything for me to do?"

"What kind of thing do you like to do?"

"I like to read. Do you have any good books?"

"We have a few. What kind do you like?"

"Thrillers mainly."

"Okay. I'll see what I can find for you."

As soon as I walked into the house, I could hear voices coming from the lounge.

"Jill! I'm in here with Kit," Jack shouted.

Big followed me through to the lounge and sat down in the corner of the room.

"What's with the trailer?" Jack said.

"I thought I'd have a bit of a clear out. I can use it to take the rubbish to the tip."

"It's only a few weeks since we had a good clear out."

"There's still plenty of stuff that needs throwing away."

"I'd better get going," Kit said. "I only came over to bring you the cake."

"Cake?" My ears pricked up.

"Britt has baked us a cake as a thank you for sponsoring them," Jack said. "Isn't that kind of her?"

"Very." Guilty conscience more like.

After Kit had left, Jack said, "Why did you really get the trailer?"

"You wouldn't believe me if I told you."

"Try me."

"Okay, but don't say that I didn't warn you. There's a giant green man sitting over there in the corner."

Jack laughed. "There's no need to be sarcastic, Jill."

"I'm not. There genuinely is a giant green man over there, but only I can see him. His name is Big."

"Hi." Big waved to Jack.

"He says hi."

"Is this a wind-up?" Jack clearly still wasn't convinced.

"No, I promise. The other day I helped an elderly lady who'd dropped her shopping. It turned out she was a fairy godmother, and to thank me, she gave me a little trinket box. It's an ugly thing, but I decided to find out what was inside it. It turned out to be a big green man."

"And he's sitting over there?"

"Correct."

"How come I can't see him?"

"No one can except for me. He's been following me around all day; he won't leave my side. When I drove to work this morning, he squashed himself into the car with me, and I could barely drive. That's why I got the trailer."

"How long is he going to stay with you?"

"I have no idea. Until I can find some way of getting rid

of him, I suppose."

"Charming," Big said.

"Sorry, but you know what I mean, big guy."

"It was nice of Britt to bake us a cake, wasn't it?" Jack said.

"Don't mention that woman to me."

"Why? What has she done to upset you?"

"Jules came by the office today; she's taking part in the marathon too. I asked her why she wasn't using the joint sponsorship form for her and Dexter. She said she thought they were unfair because people didn't realise that if they ticked the checkbox it could potentially cost them a lot more money."

"I ticked the checkbox."

"I know you did. And now if Brit and Kit both finish in three hours, we'll have to fork out ten times the amount you thought we'd sponsored them for."

"What? That's ridiculous!"

"Don't worry. I have a plan."

Chapter 13

By the time I got downstairs on Saturday morning, Jack had already finished his breakfast.

"You look dreadful," he said.

"And a very good morning to you, too. I barely got a wink of sleep last night."

"Poor you. Aren't you feeling well?"

"I'm fine, I just couldn't sleep for all the snoring."

"You should have nudged me."

"It wasn't you who was doing the snoring. It was him." I gestured towards Big, who was sitting in the corner of the kitchen. Not that Jack could see him.

"I do not snore." Big objected.

"Are you kidding me? You sounded like a road drill."

Jack still looked a little bit freaked out whenever I spoke to Big. "Couldn't you have got him to sleep in the spare bedroom?"

"Don't you think I tried? He refuses to leave my side. He even wanted to go into the bathroom with me this morning, but I drew the line there."

"What's going to happen if he snores like that every night? You'll never get any sleep again."

"I'll just have to work something out."

"At least it's Saturday. You'll be able to have a nice restful day."

"Chance would be a fine thing. Have you forgotten that I have to go to Candlefield this morning for that stupid broom flying practice?"

"Oh yeah, I had. That should be fun."

"About as much fun as lying on a bed of cacti."

"By the way, have you remembered that Dad's coming

over later?"

"Of course I have. He'll still be here when I get back won't he?"

"He should be, seeing as time stands still while you're over there."

"Yeah, but I also plan on dropping into Washbridge for the marathon."

"I didn't think you'd be interested in watching that?"

"What do you mean? I love a good marathon."

"I'll never understand you, Jill."

***

Half an hour later, after I'd finished breakfast, I told Big that I had to magic myself over to the paranormal world. "You'll have to wait for me here."

"I can't do that. I have to stay with you."

"I'm not sure if I'll be able to magic you over there because the 'shrink' spell didn't work on you. Couldn't you just stay here in the house? Time stands still here while I'm in Candlefield, so you won't even notice I'm gone."

"I can't, the rules say I have to be at your side at all times."

"Okay then, give me your hand. I'll give it a try."

This time, my magic did work on the giant green man, so I transported us both to the Range in Candlefield where broom flying practice was to be held.

"That was really cool," Big said when we arrived.

"While we're here, you'll have to keep out of the way because it could be dangerous."

"But I have to stay by your side."

"And just how do you propose to do that when I'm flying on the broom?"

He thought about it for a moment and then said, "Okay, but I'll be right here on the ground underneath you in case you fall."

"Who are you talking to, Jill?"

I turned around to find Maybelline Maytime standing there. Next to her were three other women, two of whom had been my teammates in the broom flying competition.

"Hi, Maybelline. This will probably sound crazy, but I have an invisible friend with me."

"O—kay." Maybelline raised her eyebrows. "If you say so."

"It's a long story, trust me you're better off not knowing."

"Fair enough." Maybelline turned to the other women. "You already know two of these ladies, Jill. And this is Dimples Lowe."

Dimples stepped forward and shook my hand. "I'm so pleased to meet you, Jill."

"Likewise. I'm really sorry to have taken your place in the troupe, Dimples. I honestly had no desire to."

"Don't give it another thought. I'm a long-time admirer of yours. If I had to lose my place to anyone, I'm glad it was you."

"Thanks." I turned back to Maybelline. "I can't believe Grandma is late."

"Late?" Grandma appeared from nowhere. "I'm never late!"

"Hi, Grandma. Is this practice session going to take long? It's just that I didn't get much sleep last night."

"Whose fault is that? You should tell that human of yours to leave you alone."

"What? No, it wasn't Jack. It was—err—never mind."

"And why have you brought that ugly green monster with you?"

"You can see him?"

"Of course I can see him. I could hardly miss a giant green man, could I?"

"But no-one else can. Maybelline, can you see him?"

She shook her head.

"That explains it," Grandma said.

"Explains what? Do you know who—err—what he is because if you do, I wish you'd tell me."

"Walk with me, Jill." She beckoned me to follow her. After a few yards, she turned around and said to Big, "Hey, big guy, you wait right there."

"But I have to stay next to Jill."

"I said, wait there!"

Remarkably, he did as he was told.

"Don't you realise what you have here?" she said when we were out of earshot.

"I have no idea. All I know is he came out of a trinket box."

"That makes sense. It's usually a small box or a lamp. He's a genie, obviously."

"But I asked him if he was a genie, and he said no."

"And you took him at his word?"

"Well, yeah. I also asked if he could grant me three wishes, but he said he didn't know how."

"That's because genies are both liars and lazy. And besides, why do you need wishes? You're a powerful witch, you can do anything you want."

"I just thought it would be cool."

"Give me strength. Well, he can't stay here. Not while we're practising. He'll be too much of a distraction."

"I don't know how to get rid of him."

"Did you check your spell book?"

"Err, no, but then I wouldn't know what to look for."

She grabbed her bag and took out her own copy of the spell book. "Let's see what we can find, shall we?" She flicked through a few pages. "What do you know? Here's a spell called 'How to put a genie back into a box or lamp'."

"You've just made that up." I snatched the book from her, and to my amazement, she was telling the truth. There really was such a spell. "This is great." I quickly memorised it and then handed back the book. "I can get rid of him now."

"Hurry up. We have a lot of practising to do."

"What should I do with the trinket box after he's back inside it?"

"Give it to someone else, then it's their problem."

Grandma had gone to speak to the rest of the troupe, so I collared the big green guy.

"You lied to me, Big."

"I don't know what you mean, Jill."

"Don't come the innocent. I asked if you were a genie and you said you weren't."

"I'm not. Honestly."

"I'm sorry, but I don't believe you, big guy." I cast the spell, and Big turned into a puff of green smoke, which disappeared back into the trinket box. Once he was inside, I shut the lid. Because the lock was still broken, I had to use an elastic band to stop the lid from opening again.

"Jill, let me out." The muffled voice came from inside the box. "I'm sorry. Please let me out."

I felt terrible, but I knew I had to be strong. I couldn't spend the rest of my life with a big green giant following me around; I'd never get a wink of sleep again. So, ignoring his cries for help, I put the trinket box back into my bag, and went to join the others.

Grandma handed each of us a sheet of paper on which she'd outlined the five different routines we were to practise today. Each routine was detailed in a series of lines and arrows. Two of them looked relatively straightforward, but the other three were quite complicated and would be extremely demanding. All five of us were to practise each of the routines, with one of us sitting out each time. I was pleased that Grandma had decided to include Dimples, so that she wouldn't feel left out.

The session lasted for almost two and a half hours, and by the end of it, we were all completely exhausted. Overall, I thought we'd done a remarkable job, but of course Grandma was less than impressed.

"I'd better get going now," I said.

"Hold your horses." Grandma caught me by the arm. "Not so quick. We haven't finished yet."

"Why not? You said we all had to practise each of the routines, and we've done that. I need to get back to Washbridge."

"Here she is." Grandma pointed to a young witch who was headed our way. "Bang on time."

"Who's that?"

"This, Jill, is your choreographer, Millie Martin."

"*Choreographer*? Why do we need a choreographer? We're riding brooms."

"This is not just broom flying, Jill. It's synchronised broom flying, and it's supposed to be artistic. That's where the choreography comes in."

"Are you kidding me? It's already difficult enough to stay on the brooms while we're doing these routines. Do you really expect us to do some kind of weird dancing at the same time?"

"It's not like I'm asking you to tap dance. You'll just be moving your upper body and arms around in a synchronised way."

"But I have no sense of rhythm."

"Rubbish." Grandma turned to Millie. "This is Maybelline Maytime, the troupe leader. She'll introduce you to everyone else. I have to nip off for a few minutes, but I'll be back shortly to watch you perform."

"I'm very pleased to meet you all," Millie said, after Maybelline had made the introductions. "How many of you have danced before?"

Everyone put their hands up. Everyone, that is, apart from me.

"Not even when you were a child, Jill?"

"No. My sister, Kathy, was into that kind of thing, but not me."

"It's okay. You'll pick it up very quickly. And the good news is that you won't have to do anything in the air until you've mastered the routines here on the ground. Now, if you would all stand in a line and follow me."

Millie had brought a CD player with her (who still used those things?). Everyone else seemed to find the routines easy to follow, but not me. I was all over the place. I had my right arm up when it should've been my left. I had both arms in the air when they should've been by my sides. I swayed to the left when I should've swayed to the right. All in all, I was completely useless. Midway through the second of the routines, Grandma came back. It didn't help having her watching my every (wrong) move.

The whole thing took almost another hour. By the end of it, I was practically on my knees with exhaustion.

"That's it for today," Millie said. "Thank you, ladies." She picked up the CD player and made her way out of the Range.

"What did you think?" Maybelline asked Grandma.

"I thought that four-fifths of you were very good." She turned her gaze on me. "And then there was you."

"I'm sorry, but I've never done any dancing before. I'm not very good."

"You've got that right. Dimples, you're back in the first team."

***

Washbridge city centre was as busy as I'd ever seen it. There were thousands of people gathered all along the route of the marathon, to cheer on the runners. My reason for being there, though, was slightly different.

I managed to work my way to the halfway point of the course, and I planned to wait there until I saw Britt and Kit run by. I didn't have long to wait. By my calculations, if they kept up the same pace for the second half of the race, they'd both finish well inside three hours.

As they ran past, I gave them both a little wave.

"Hi, Jill," Britt shouted.

"Good luck," I shouted back. They were going to need it. Snigger.

***

When I arrived home, I expected to find Jack's dad still there, but there was no sign of him.

"Where's Roy?"

"He went home early."

"Oh dear. I hope you didn't upset him with talk of your mother."

"Quite the contrary. He wasn't very receptive to the idea at first, but in the end, I managed to persuade him to give it a go. And what do you know, it worked out brilliantly."

"Did he actually speak to Yvonne?"

"He did; they talked for almost twenty minutes. I stayed with them for a while, but then I left them to it."

"That's fantastic."

"When Mum finally broke the connection, Dad was like a different man. Just like he used to be before she died. I'm so glad you persuaded me to do this, Jill."

"Do you think they'll keep in touch?"

"There's no doubt about that. Dad was talking about them having regular chinwags in the evenings."

"That's fantastic. I couldn't be happier for him. And for you, of course."

"What about your day? How did the broom flying go?"

"Grandma has kicked me out of the team."

"Oh dear. I'm sorry."

"Don't be. I was thrilled when she dropped me."

"Why did she?"

"Because my dancing skills didn't cut it."

"*Dancing?* How can you dance on a broomstick?"

"We were expected to move our arms and upper body around while flying."

"That's ridiculous."

"You're telling me. She brought in a choreographer to train us, but I was completely hopeless. When Grandma saw how bad I was, she kicked me off the team and replaced me with Dimples Lowe."

"Are you sure you're okay with that?"

"I couldn't be happier."

Jack glanced around the room. "Is your big green friend here?"

"Big? No, he's gone."

"Gone where?"

"I hate to admit it, but I have Grandma to thank for getting rid of him. It turned out he was a genie after all. He'd totally lied to me about it."

"So where is he now?"

"Back in his trinket box. Grandma found a spell to put him back in there."

"The poor guy."

"Never mind *poor guy*. You wouldn't be saying that if you had a big green man following you around all the time, keeping you awake all night with his snoring."

"True. Where's the trinket box now?"

"I left it with Grandma."

I didn't dare risk telling Jack that the trinket box was actually at the bottom of my bag, in case he felt sorry for Big and let him out.

"Did you watch the marathon?" Jack asked.

"Yeah, but not for long. I did see Britt and Kit run past."

"How were they doing?"

"They were going well, setting quite a pace."

"That's not good news. It could end up costing us a small fortune."

"Somehow, I don't think so."

"Why not?"

"I just have a feeling that they may find the second half of the marathon harder than the first."

"Why do I get the feeling there's something you're not telling me?"

"I have no idea what you're talking about. Anyway, what's for dinner? I'm starving."

Chapter 14

It was Monday morning, and I felt much more with it. I'd spent most of Sunday in bed; it had been fantastic to be able to sleep without having to listen to someone snoring on the floor beside me.

I still felt a little guilty, knowing that Big was trapped in the trinket box in my bag, but not guilty enough to consider letting him out. I consoled myself with the fact that he'd previously been in there for hundreds of years, and he'd seemed perfectly happy. Another few days until I found him a new home didn't seem unreasonable to me. The problem was where would that new home be? Who could I give the trinket box to? The thing was seriously ugly, so I'd need to find someone who had no taste whatsoever.

"Good morning, darling." Jack gave me a kiss on the cheek when I came downstairs. "You look a lot better today."

"I feel much better, thanks. I just wish it wasn't Monday. I feel as though I've only had a one-day weekend."

"If you think you feel bad, just spare a thought for poor old Big. I can't help but feel sorry for the big guy."

"Don't do that, Jack. I don't need you to guilt trip me. What else could I do?"

"I know you're right, but it just seems kind of weird thinking of him inside that small box. It must be so claustrophobic."

"That's enough, Jack."

"Sorry. I had a phone call from Dad a couple of minutes ago."

"At this time in the morning? Is he okay?"

"He's great. Apparently, he and mum had a long chat yesterday, and he's absolutely buzzing."

"That's fantastic. I'm really pleased for you."

We'd no sooner finished breakfast than there was a knock at the door. Why do people insist on coming to the house at this time of the morning? Have they got nothing better to do? We both went through to the hallway, and Jack answered the door to find Britt standing there.

"Morning, you two. I hope you don't mind me calling around so early, but I'm hoping to collect all the sponsorship money as soon as possible. Only if it's convenient, of course."

"Yeah, come in, Britt," I said. "How did it go yesterday?"

"Not too well, Jill. The first half was fine; we were setting a great pace."

"You seemed to be going well when I saw you both. I assumed you'd go on to set a personal best time."

"So did we, but then everything went wrong in the second half."

"Why? What happened?"

"That's just it, I don't know. I slowed down to a walking pace. It was as though I had lead weights in my shoes. I could barely lift my legs."

"Did you have cramp?" Jack said.

"No, it definitely wasn't cramp. I've had cramp lots of times, and it's never felt like that. My feet just felt so heavy."

"What about Kit?" I asked. "Did he go on without you?"

"No, he felt exactly the same. It took us over four hours to finish. We've never run so slowly."

"That is weird," Jack said, clearly struggling to keep a straight face.

"So, how much do we owe you, Britt?" I asked.

"As we didn't both finish in under three hours, it's just the basic amount you sponsored us for."

After Britt had left, Jack said, "What did you do?"

"Me? Nothing."

"Come on, Jill. Tell me."

"Okay. I may have cast a spell that made their running shoes feel like deep sea diver boots."

"I should be mad at you." He laughed. "But that's just too funny."

***

When I arrived at the toll bridge, Mr Ivers was looking even sadder than he had on Saturday, and I wouldn't have believed that was possible.

"Good morning, Mr Ivers. How are you today?"

"Oh, you know, Jill. Pretty much the same."

And that's when I had a brilliant idea.

"I expect you're still feeling a little down because of Ivy."

"You're right. I am."

"I was in town the other day, and I saw this and thought you might like it." I took the trinket box out of my bag, quickly slipped off the elastic band, and handed the box to him. "It's only a little thing, but it's very nice to look at, don't you think?"

"It's beautiful, Jill." His face lit up. "That's so very kind of you. No one ever buys me presents. What is it, exactly?"

"It's a trinket box."

"What's inside?"

"No! Whatever you do, you mustn't open it."

"Why not?"

"The lady in the shop told me that it's bad luck to look inside. But it's a really nice thing just to put on a shelf and admire, don't you think?"

"It is. Thanks again. That's really kind of you. Look, why don't you just pay for the car this time. There's no need to pay for the trailer."

"Thank you."

What were the chances that Mr Ivers wouldn't open the trinket box? Zero, I'd estimate, but that was okay because he was short on friends, and he'd appreciate Big's company. And the big guy would just be happy to be free again. Overall, I figured I deserved a pat on the back for having done my good deed for the day.

***

En-route into town, I called into Washbridge Trailer Rental, to return and pay for the CarryAll 673. The sales assistant asked if I'd managed to transport the tall telephone box, and I assured him that all had gone well.

In the office building, the two clowns were still staring down the stairs at me. Hopefully, Jimmy and I would be able to come to a friendly compromise before the day was out.

Mrs V was humming away to herself and looked as happy as a lark.

"Good morning, Mrs V, you're looking exceptionally pleased with life this morning."

"I feel completely rested today." She looked around as though she thought someone might be eavesdropping. "Between you and me, Armi seems to have settled down a little in *that* department."

"Oh? O—kay. That's a good thing I'm guessing?"

"Absolutely. We had a lovely little picnic yesterday. It was delightful."

"Did you and Armi eat any apples?"

"Apples? No, actually I had a banana and he had an orange. Why do you ask?"

"No reason. For some reason, I was just thinking about apples."

When I went through to my office, I was relieved to find that all the broadcasting equipment had been removed. Winky was lying on the sofa and looked only half awake.

"Good morning, Winky. I didn't wake you, did I?"

He sat up, stretched and yawned. "I've had a busy weekend. Do you know how heavy that equipment is that you made me move?"

"It's your own fault for bringing it up here in the first place. What have you done with it?"

"I decided that running a radio station wasn't a good use of my time. It was fun while it lasted, but it was never going to make me any money, so I've passed on the mantle to Hubert the Ham."

"Does he have a particular taste for meat?"

"No. It's *ham* as in radio ham. Hubert knows everything there is to know about radio and broadcasting. I agreed that he could rename the station to Ham FM, and that I'll receive twenty percent of all advertising income."

As I sat at my desk and went through the morning's post, Winky began to look all around the room. "Where is he?"

"Where's who?"

"The jolly green —"

"Big? He's gone."

"Like he was ever here in the first place."

"I don't expect you to believe this, but it turned out that Big is actually a genie. Anyway, I managed to put him back into the trinket box."

"A genie, eh? And did he grant you any wishes?"

"No, he actually told me he wasn't a genie. Such a liar."

"You do realise that you sound like a complete nutjob, don't you?"

After speaking to Sylvia Long, I now knew that Edward Broom had disappeared sometime after their dinner out. They'd apparently had a blazing row and she'd stormed out of the restaurant. Other than that, I had absolutely nothing to go on, so in the absence of any other leads, I decided to take a closer look at the similar cases that had occurred over the last couple of years. One thing that struck me was that all the people who had disappeared had been wealthy. Even more curious, was that they'd all stayed in budget hotels. It was quite possible that one or two of them might have been a little tight with the purse strings, but it seemed unlikely that they would all have elected to spend the night in a downmarket hotel.

I had nothing to lose by trying to contact the partners of the people who had disappeared, so I started with one of the more recent cases: Three months earlier, a man by the name of Alan Bowler had disappeared from a hotel in Cambridge. It didn't take long to track down an address and contact number for his wife, Margaret. When I called her, she readily agreed to talk to me, so I arranged to go down there later that day.

Mrs V poked her head around the door.

"Jill, I have the gentleman from Clown to see you."

"Good. Send him in, would you?"

Jimmy was dressed in full clown costume. As soon as Winky spotted him, he disappeared under the sofa.

"Do have a seat, Jimmy."

"Actually, it's Breezy when I'm in costume."

"Yes, of course, sorry. Do have a seat, *Breezy*."

He struggled to get his enormous clown feet under the desk, but he eventually managed it.

"Sneezy tells me that you're unhappy with our new sign, Jill."

"That's correct, Breezy, and I'm sure you must see why."

"I don't, actually. It's just a sign with two clowns on it, and everyone loves clowns."

"Not everyone, Breezy, but that's not really the point, is it? When your customers come into the building, I'm sure they're delighted to see those clowns, but you also have to take account of my clients. When they visit these offices, it's usually to discuss matters of a very serious nature: missing persons, thefts, even murders. What kind of impression will they get if the first thing they see when they walk through the door is two clowns staring down at them?"

"Look, Jill. I really don't want us to fall out over this. I'm more than happy to discuss a compromise."

"I'm glad to hear you say that, Breezy. What did you have in mind?"

"How about I change the size of the sign so you can't see it from the bottom of the stairs?"

"That's rather missing the point, though, isn't it? As soon as my clients get to the top of the stairs, they'll still see the clowns."

"Okay, how about I change the sign so there's only one clown?"

"Once again, Breezy, that doesn't really solve the problem, does it?"

"I'm sorry, Jill, but I'm simply not prepared to fork out for yet another sign; not when the one that's out there is perfectly okay."

"I don't think it is perfectly okay. I think it's monstrous."

"If that's your attitude, there's nothing else to talk about." He stood up. "You're being totally unreasonable. It's all take and no give with you."

"That's ridiculous. I'm the most reasonable person you could ever hope to do business with."

"I have nothing more to say on the matter. From now on, please submit your complaints through my solicitor." And with that, he stormed out of the office.

As soon as he'd gone, Winky came out from under the sofa. "That went well."

"Be quiet, you. Anyway, I thought you weren't scared of clowns."

"I'm not."

"Then why did you hide under the sofa just now?"

"I wasn't hiding. It's just cooler under there."

***

I'd driven all the way down to and parked on the road outside Mrs Bowler's house. It was a large detached bungalow with a beautiful garden.

I was halfway up her drive when a ginger tom cat came running across the lawn and planted himself on the path in front of me.

"What are you doing here?" he demanded.

"Excuse me, but I don't think that's any of your business."

"It is my business because this is my gaff."

"I take it by that you live here."

"That's what I just said, isn't it? It's my gaff."

"I'm here to see your owner, Margaret Bowler."

"Excuse me, but I don't have an *owner*."

I should have known better than to say that; it always upset Winky if I referred to myself as his owner.

"Sorry, I'll rephrase that. I'm here to see Margaret Bowler, who I believe shares this house with you."

"And who might you be?"

"I don't see that's any of your business."

"Unless you tell me, you will not pass."

"Is that right?"

I took a step forward and he lunged at me with his claws bared. I only just managed to pull my leg back in time.

"Hey, there was no need for that."

I was just considering which spell to use on the horrible creature when the door of the bungalow opened.

"Timmikins, move out of the way so the lady can get by you."

Timmikins? I laughed "What kind of name is that?" I said to him in a hushed voice.

"I didn't choose it."

"Do as the lady says, and step aside."

"I will not."

"I'm Jill Maxwell," I shouted to the woman at the door.

"Hello, Jill. I'm very sorry about Timmikins; he can be a little antisocial sometimes. Now, Timmikins, do as you're told and move out of the way."

The ginger tom shot me a final look, and then stepped to one side and allowed me to pass.

"Do come in, Jill, I was just about to put the kettle on. Is tea okay for you?"

"Tea would be lovely, thank you."

Once we had our drinks, we made our way through to a beautiful room at the rear of the property, which overlooked a large garden.

"Thank you for agreeing to see me today, Mrs Bowler."

"Please call me Margaret."

"I wondered if you might have any idea what happened to your husband?"

"I don't know where he is, if that's what you mean, but I'm pretty sure the whole thing was planned."

"Really? You think he deliberately vanished?"

"Yes, and I told the police as much. Not that they took a blind bit of notice."

"What makes you say that?"

"It's quite simple. I'd had enough of the man and had told him I wanted a divorce. That would have meant I got half of everything."

"But surely, after he disappeared, you got it *all*, didn't you?"

"On the face of it, yes, but Andrew was very cunning and secretive. I'd always suspected that he had bank accounts I knew nothing about. In fact, I stumbled across one of them after he disappeared. Unfortunately, there was no money left in it because he transferred out a quarter of a million just a few days before he vanished."

"Who did he send the money to?"

"That, I don't know. The only thing I have is the account number where he sent the money. I've asked my bank and the police, but no one seems willing or able to trace it."

"Do you think you could let me have a note of the account number?"

"Yes, of course. I'll give it to you before you leave."

"There's one thing that puzzles me. Clearly, you and your husband are quite well-to-do, and yet your husband was staying at a budget hotel when he disappeared. Is that something he was in the habit of doing?"

"Absolutely not. The idea is ridiculous. Andrew would no more have stayed at a budget hotel than he would have slept on the streets."

Chapter 15

It was a long drive back from Cambridge and I was absolutely starving, so I pulled into a roadside cafe called the Two o'clock Rock and Roll Diner.

Unusual name.

It was very quiet inside, and the staff seemed to outnumber the customers two to one. I took a seat and checked the menu, which wasn't very exciting, but I was so hungry that I would have eaten anything. When the waitress came to take my order, I opted for a hot dog and fries.

"I'm curious. Why is this place called the Two o'clock Rock and Roll Diner?"

She smiled and checked her watch. "You'll find out soon enough." And then off she went without another word.

I thought no more about it and got stuck into my meal, such as it was. I'd just finished when the clock on the wall struck two. Then everything went crazy: The jukebox, which had stood silent at one end of the diner, suddenly burst into life and began to blast out a rock and roll classic. The staff jumped onto the counter and tables and began to dance. Even the customers suddenly stood up and joined in.

I couldn't believe my eyes.

A man in his forties who was seated at a table two down from me, got out of his seat and walked over to my table.

"May I have this dance?"

"I'm sorry, but I can't dance."

"Don't be silly. Everyone can dance."

He took my hand, pulled me to my feet, and the next thing I knew, we were dancing. He spun me around, and even threw me through his legs and over his shoulders.

The weird thing was, I kind of enjoyed it. This went on for two more records before the jukebox fell silent again. The staff all returned to their serving duties, and the customers went back to their meals.

The man who had been dancing with me thanked me. "I thought you said you couldn't dance?"

"I – err – "

"You were great and don't let anyone tell you otherwise."

"Thanks. Does that happen often? The dancing, I mean?"

"Twice a day, at two in the afternoon and then again at two in the morning."

"Two in the morning?"

"Yeah, this place is open twenty-four hours. Did you enjoy yourself?"

"Yes, I did."

***

When I arrived back at the office, someone had drawn moustaches on both of the clowns, and had written 'All Clowns Stink' across the sign. Although I would never condone vandalism, I agreed wholeheartedly with the sentiment.

Waiting for me in the outer office, was someone I'd hoped never to see again.

"Gordon? What do you want?"

The law firm of Armitage, Armitage, Armitage and

Poole had once occupied the offices next-door to mine, where Clown were now based. Gordon Armitage had done his best to get me evicted from my office, but he'd failed miserably.

"It's very nice to see you too, Jill."

"I asked what you wanted?"

"I'm here on official business, actually." He took an envelope out of his briefcase and handed it to me.

"What's this?"

"I'm serving these papers on you on behalf of my client."

"And who on earth is your client?"

"The company just down the corridor from here."

"Clown?"

"That's correct."

"What are the papers? What's this all about, Gordon?"

"They're suing you for criminal damage."

"What do you mean, criminal damage? What am I supposed to have done?"

"You defaced their property. Vis-a-vis the sign just outside the door."

"I didn't have anything to do with that."

"But you would say that, wouldn't you? From what I remember, you and the truth have always been distant friends."

If Mrs V hadn't been there, I'd have turned him into a cockroach there and then, and taken great pleasure in crushing it under my foot.

"I'll see you in court, Jill." And with that, he left.

"Oh dear, Jill." Mrs V was clearly shocked by what had just transpired. "What have you done?"

"Me? I haven't done anything."

"Right."

"Don't you believe me?"

"Of course I do, dear, but you were very angry about that sign."

Great. If Mrs V didn't believe in my innocence, what were the chances of my convincing the courts?

In my office, Winky was running around like a crazy cat, and it took me a couple of minutes to work out what he was doing.

"You'll never catch that moth. You're way too slow."

He came to a halt next to my desk. "Who are you calling slow?" He gasped.

"You can barely catch your breath. You're out of shape."

"That's rich coming from you."

"Hey, I'll have you know that I've just been jiving."

"Don't be ridiculous." He laughed.

"It's true. On the way back from Cambridge, I stopped at a diner and I was jiving with the best of them."

"You are completely delusional. It was bad enough when you thought you were talking to a big green man, but the idea that you could jive is way crazier. Anyway, what was all that kerfuffle out there, just now?"

"That was our dear old friend, Gordon Armitage."

"What did he want?"

"To serve these papers on me."

"What have you done now? Is someone suing you for throwing stuff out of the window?"

"Those clowns down the corridor have accused me of defacing their sign."

"Those moustaches are funny," he laughed.

"How do you know about the moustaches?"

He shrugged. "Just an educated guess."

"You did it, didn't you?"

"Not guilty, your honour."

Winky continued to insist he'd had nothing to do with the defacing of the sign, but I wasn't entirely sure I believed him. Still, I didn't have time to worry about that because I had to go over to GT to speak to Lily, who I'd met at the bridge club.

***

"Lily. I don't know if you remember me, but we met—"

"Of course I do. It's Jill, isn't it? Is Madge all right?"

"Yes, she's fine, as far as I know."

"Would you like to come in?"

"Yes, please."

She led the way into the living room, which appeared to be a shrine to all things dolphin. There were pictures of them on every wall, and dolphin ornaments of all sizes on every available surface.

"I see you're keen on dolphins."

"Yes, ever since I was a child. I used to love to swim with them, but unfortunately that's not possible here in GT. So, Jill, what was it you wanted to talk to me about?"

"When I met you at the bridge club, you mentioned something about your jewellery going missing."

"That's right, but I'm pretty sure I've misplaced it somewhere. It'll turn up sooner or later."

"How long has it been missing?"

"A few weeks, I suppose. Why do you ask? Do you think someone is actually stealing jewellery?"

"I don't know, but it's possible. What is it that has gone missing?"

"A locket necklace."

"Is it valuable?"

"Not particularly. Just sentimental value really. My husband, Bill, gave it to me."

"Is Bill here in GT?"

"No, he's still alive."

"Have you ever made contact with him since — err — ?"

"I died?" She smiled. "It's okay, you're allowed to say it. No. Bill is a bit old fashioned. He never did believe in ghosts or anything like that. I considered trying to get in touch with him when I first arrived here, but I thought I'd be wasting my time. And, to be perfectly honest, we never really had much to talk about when I was alive."

"Lily, would you mind if I paid him a visit?"

"No, but why would you want to do that? Is it to do with the missing jewellery?"

"Yeah, I'm just working on a hunch at the moment. It's a bit of a longshot that will probably prove to be nothing, but it would be helpful if I could speak to him."

"Go ahead. I have no objections."

"Thanks. Is there anything you'd like me to tell him? Any message you'd like me to give him?"

"Just tell him I hope he's remembering to change his vest more than once a week."

I had hoped that Lily might offer me a drink, but it hadn't seemed to occur to her, and of course, I was far too polite to suggest it. By the time I left her house, I was desperate for a coffee, so I decided to drop in at Cakey C.

Mum and Dad were both in the shop, and

unsurprisingly, neither of them was working. Yvonne appeared to be manning the counter by herself while my parents were at a table near the back of the shop, both staring intently at a pile of paperwork.

Neither of them had noticed me when I entered the shop.

"Hi, Jill," Yvonne said. "How are you?"

"Very well, thanks. How come you're running the place single-handed?"

"I'm not supposed to be." She glanced over at my parents. "The person who was supposed to be helping me didn't show up for work today, and it doesn't look like anyone else is going to step in and help."

"I can have a word with them if you like?"

"No, don't do that. I finish in ten minutes, anyway."

"Okay. I hear you managed to get in touch with Roy."

"That's right. I did." I'd expected her to be excited, but her response was somewhat subdued.

"Is everything okay, Yvonne?"

"Yes, of course."

"Are you sure? I expected you to be on top of the world after speaking to Roy."

"Could we talk when I've done behind here? It'll only be a few minutes now."

"Yes, of course."

"What can I get you in the meantime?"

"A caramel latte and something to eat. What would you suggest?"

"The lemon drizzle cake is lovely."

"Okay, I'll try a piece of that."

Once I had my drink and cake, I decided I should go and say hello to Mum and Dad who still hadn't noticed I was there.

"Hey, you two. I was beginning to think you were ignoring me."

"Sorry, Jill," Mum said. "I didn't notice you come in."

"What are you two so engrossed in?"

"These are our new plans for the shop," Dad said.

"I thought this place was doing really well."

"It is," Mum said. "But in business, Jill, you can't afford to stand still. If you do, you're finished. As a businesswoman, you must realise that, surely."

"Of course. Absolutely. So, what are you planning to do exactly?"

"The first thing we're going to do is to install a chocolate fountain." Dad handed me a brochure.

Oh, no. This was déjà vu.

"I'm not sure that's such a good idea."

"Why ever not, Jill?" Mum was clearly disappointed by my reaction. "People love chocolate and those fountains look great. They're bound to bring more people into the shop."

"Yes, but you have to be very careful with them. They can cause havoc."

"What do you mean?"

"Amber and Pearl installed a chocolate fountain in Cuppy C some time ago, and it turned out to be an unmitigated disaster."

"In what way?"

"The thing overflowed and flooded the shop with chocolate. The floor was covered in it."

Mum looked horrified. "Maybe we should shelve that idea."

"I think you're right," Dad said. "We have other

exciting plans we can focus on."

"Such as?"

"We're thinking of installing a conveyor belt."

Ten minutes later, I'd managed to persuade my parents that they should also abandon the conveyor belt idea.

Having finished her shift, Yvonne came to join me at a table near the window and Mum and Dad took over behind the counter.

"What's wrong, Yvonne? I thought you'd be over the moon about seeing Roy again."

"I am, Jill. It was lovely."

"Why do I sense a 'but' coming?"

"It's just that he kept asking me about my life here in ghost town."

"That's only natural, isn't it?"

"Yes, of course, and I understand that, but when I told him that I was working here, he didn't seem very happy about it."

"Why ever not?"

"I was pretty much a stay-at-home mother and housewife after Jack was born."

"Apart from the whole witchfinder thing?"

"Well, yes, but Roy knew nothing about that."

"I don't see what difference it should make to him if you want to work now that you're here in ghost town."

"Neither do I. And the other thing was that he kept asking me if I was seeing anyone."

"Another man, you mean?"

"Yeah. I told him I wasn't, but I'm not sure he believed me. I think he was jealous."

"That's just silly. Shall I have a word with Jack?"

"No, please don't do that, Jill. I wouldn't want to worry him. It's nothing. I'm sure it'll blow over soon enough."

Chapter 16

Jack hadn't got back by the time I went to bed last night, so I hadn't had the chance to talk to him about his father. Yvonne had told me that I shouldn't say anything, but I figured Jack had a right to know.

We were at the kitchen table eating breakfast (or in Jack's case, what passed for breakfast).

"What time did you get in last night?" I said.

"After midnight."

"More vandalism in the school toilet block?"

"No. Actually, we had a hostage situation."

"Another one?"

"Yeah, who'd have thought it. Thankfully, everything turned out okay."

"What happened?"

"A guy was holding his wife at knifepoint, threatening to kill her."

"Is she all right?"

"Yes. Just after midnight she walked out of the door by herself, unharmed."

"What about him?"

"He'd fallen asleep and dropped the knife. Apparently, he'd been drinking all day. Once he'd dozed off, his wife simply got up and left."

"He sounds like an idiot."

"Thank goodness he was. It could have ended a lot worse."

"Any idea what sparked it?"

"It seems his wife had told him she was leaving him, and he saw red."

"I didn't hear you come to bed."

"That's because you were dead to the world, and snoring."

"I don't snore."

"O—kay." He grinned.

"I do not. I saw your mum yesterday."

"Where?"

"I was in GT, so I dropped into Cakey C. She was by herself behind the counter."

"How was she coping?"

"Okay. She seems to have got the hang of it now."

"I bet she was over the moon that she'd spoken to Dad, wasn't she?"

"Err, yeah, I think so."

"You don't sound very sure. What did she say?"

"That I shouldn't say anything to you."

"You have to tell me now. What's happened?"

"She was obviously pleased to have made contact with your dad, but it sounds like he gave her a bit of a hard time."

"How do you mean?"

"According to Yvonne, he wasn't very happy that she was working."

"Why not?"

"She reckoned that Roy was used to her being a stay-at-home mum and housewife, and that he'd never liked the idea of her going out to work."

"That's ridiculous."

"That's what I said. She also got the impression that he might be a little jealous."

"Of what?"

"There's nothing to be jealous of, but apparently he asked if she was seeing anyone."

"She isn't, is she?"

"No, but I can't see what business it would be of his if she was. Can you?"

Jack hesitated a little too long.

"Jack?"

"It's complicated, isn't it?"

"How is it complicated? Your father's free to start a new relationship here in the human world. Why shouldn't she be free to do the same?"

"I guess so. I'd never had to think about this kind of stuff until you introduced me to the paranormal and ghosts. I find it really hard to get my head around it."

To be fair, Jack was right. It was complicated, and made me dizzy just thinking about it, so I changed the subject. "Have you made any progress on that missing person case of yours?"

"Not really, but there is one odd aspect of the case that's bugging me: The guy who went missing was quite wealthy, and yet for some reason he chose to stay in a budget hotel in West Chipping. It's not like there aren't any five-star hotels there. That seems kind of weird to me."

"It's funny you should say that because I looked into a number of similar cases dating back a few years, and I found the exact same thing. Several of the people who went missing were wealthy, and yet they all disappeared from budget hotels. That can't possibly be a coincidence, can it?"

***

This was just too funny. So funny, in fact, that I almost

crashed the car. The toll booth was very small, and there was barely enough room to accommodate Mr Ivers and his new green friend. Mr Ivers was squashed up against the glass, but it obviously didn't bother him because he had a huge smile on his face. That was something I hadn't seen for a while.

"Good morning, Jill." He beamed. "Isn't it a beautiful day today?"

"It certainly is, Mr Ivers. And you're looking remarkably happy, I must say."

"Why wouldn't I be? The sun is out, the sky is blue, and all is well with the world. And that gift you gave me certainly helped, Jill. It's nice to know that someone cares."

"Think nothing of it. I'm pleased you like it, but I hope you haven't opened the box."

"Of course not," he lied. "I promised that I wouldn't, and I'm a man of my word."

Big was looking through the glass, but he didn't acknowledge me. I wasn't sure if going back in the trinket box had caused him to forget who I was, or if he was just blanking me. I wasn't sure why I could still see him; perhaps I possessed the same powers as Grandma.

**

When I arrived at the office building, the defaced clown sign had disappeared.

Result!

I was just about to go through to my office when I heard someone coming up the stairs; it was Jimmy and Kimmy. I considered ducking inside, but why should I?

It's not like I'd done anything wrong.

"We have nothing to say to you, Jill," Jimmy said.

"Well, I have something to say to you two. I know we've had our disagreements, but I did not deface your sign."

"Do you seriously expect us to believe that?"

"Yes, I do because it happens to be the truth."

"Well, someone defaced it, and that someone will have to pay."

"Speaking of which, your solicitor, Gordon Armitage, paid me a visit yesterday."

"I'm sorry, Jill." Jimmy grabbed Kimmy by the arm. "We're not prepared to discuss this any further. We'll see you in court." And with that, the two of them disappeared down the corridor.

Charming. And after all the things I'd done for them.

Mrs V was at her desk, wearing a cute little hat. In all the years I'd known her, I couldn't remember her wearing a hat more than a couple of times, and certainly not whilst seated at her desk. There was another woman, also wearing a hat, sitting next to her.

"Good morning, Jill," Mrs V said. "This is Hattie Hattersley."

"I'm very pleased to meet you, Jill." Hattie stood up and shook my hand. She seemed to be staring at my head. "I see you're not wearing a hat."

"I rarely do."

"If you don't mind me saying so, an outfit isn't complete without a hat."

"Hattie's a milliner," Mrs V said. "We go way back, but I haven't seen her for a number of years."

"I only recently moved back up here," Hattie said. "I've just opened a little shop close to the marketplace."

"Hattie's Hats?"

"Actually, no. It's called Hattersley's Milliners, but I wish I'd thought of that. It has a certain ring to it. You really must pop in some time, Jill."

"Maybe, but like I said, I'm not really big on hats. Anyway, I'll leave you two to *hat*."

Winky was sitting on my desk, and he was wearing what looked like a grey trilby.

"What's that thing on your head?"

"I'm sure that even *you* can work that out."

"Why are you wearing a hat?"

"Haven't you heard, Jill? An outfit isn't complete without one."

"Don't you start. I've got enough on with Hattie out there."

Just then, a pretty white cat, wearing a pink collar, appeared at the window.

"Are you ready, Winky?" she said.

"I was born ready." He jumped off the desk, scurried across the floor, and jumped into the window beside her.

"Aren't you going to introduce me?" I said.

He turned around, gave me a dismissive look and said, "No."

Mid-morning, Mrs V came through to my office. "There's a young lady out there, Jill. She says her name is Rebecca, and that you know her."

"Rebecca? I don't think so."

"Apparently, she's your accountant's lady friend?"

"Of course. Would you send her in, please?"

"Is everything okay, Rebecca? Nothing's happened to Luther, has it?"

"No, he's fine. I hope you don't mind me popping in like this."

"Not at all. What can I do for you?"

"As you've probably already realised, Luther and I have really hit it off."

"He certainly gave me that impression."

"Obviously, he isn't aware of my little secret."

"That you're a werewolf? Is that likely to cause a problem?"

"I didn't think so until we met you the other day, and he suggested that the four of us go for a meal on Friday."

"How do you mean?"

"It's a full moon that day."

"Oh dear. I thought you looked a little on edge at the time."

"He caught me off-guard; I didn't know what to say. I could hardly tell him the truth, could I? I don't know what to do, Jill. I don't want to do anything that might get me into trouble with the rogue retrievers."

"I can put your mind at ease on that score. I regularly work with the rogue retrievers, and I can promise you they have bigger fish to fry. And don't worry about the dinner date. How about I call Luther and tell him that something's cropped up at our end, and suggest we rearrange it for the week after. Would that work for you?"

"That would be great. Are you sure you don't mind doing that? I don't want to put you in a difficult position."

"It's no problem. I'll be happy to do it. How long have you lived in Washbridge, Rebecca?"

"A couple of years now."

"Do you like it here in the human world?"

"Yes, and it's even better since I met Luther."

"Where do you live?"

"Those new apartments near the cinema."

"I know the ones. They look nice."

"They are. I like it there. At least, I did until the last week or so."

"Why, what's happened?"

"Some new neighbours have moved in, and they're a little rowdy. They've been causing a bit of upset."

"Is it anything I can help with?"

"No, it's nothing. I'm sure it'll all blow over soon. I'd better get going. Thanks again, Jill."

"No problem. I'll give Luther a call later, to tell him that Jack has to work on Friday night, and suggest we make it the following week."

***

Lily wasn't sure if her husband, Bill, lived in the same house they'd shared together, but she said she thought it was likely, if only because he would be too lazy to move house.

It turned out she was right: He still lived in the same semi-detached house that they'd shared for over thirty years. The man who answered the door had wispy grey hair and was wearing odd slippers.

"I don't buy anything at the door," he snapped.

"That's okay. I'm not here to sell you anything, Bill."

"How do you know my name?"

"I'm working alongside the police at the moment," I

lied. "We're going house to house to warn people that there's someone going around selling jewellery, which supposedly once belonged to a loved one who has recently passed away."

"That still doesn't explain how you know my name."

He had a point.

"Err, the police have compiled a list of everyone who has lost a loved one within the last few years."

"But, it's over *ten* years since I lost my Lily."

Oh bum!

"Right, anyway, as I was saying, I just wanted to warn you that if someone comes to the door and says that they're selling jewellery which belonged to your — err, did you say Lily?"

"That's right."

"If anyone does call, don't buy anything from them."

"You're too late, girl. A guy came around here a couple of weeks ago, selling jewellery."

"You didn't buy anything, did you?"

"I did, but only because I recognised it. I bought that locket and chain for Lily when we were young."

"Didn't you wonder how he came by it?"

"Of course I did, but he wouldn't tell me. He asked if I wanted the jewellery or not. Said he could always find another buyer if I didn't, so I gave him the cash."

"Did you think of calling the police afterwards?"

"What good would that have done? They don't have time to investigate anything these days."

"Would it be possible for me to take a photo of the jewellery you bought?"

"If you like. You'd best come inside."

He led the way into the kitchen. "Sit yourself down

there. I'll go and get it for you."

He disappeared upstairs and returned a few minutes later.

"There you are. Pretty, isn't it?" He put the locket onto the table.

"It's lovely." I took out my phone and snapped a couple of photos.

"Would you like a cuppa while you're here?"

"Err, no thanks. I really do need to get going."

"I miss her, you know," he said, as he showed me out. "My Lily. She used to drive me crazy when she was alive, but the house seems empty without her."

"Can I ask you a bit of a weird question, Bill?"

"Fire away. You won't be the first one to do it."

"Do you happen to believe in ghosts?"

"Don't be stupid, girl. There's no such thing."

"What if I told you that you might be able to speak to your Lily again?"

"I'd say you been at the pop."

Chapter 17

As soon as I'd left Bill, I magicked myself to Ghost Town to see Lily.

"I didn't expect to see you again so soon, Jill."

"I've just been speaking to Bill."

"How is he?"

"He's fine. As you suspected, he's still living in the same house. He said that he was missing you."

"Did he really? Or are you just saying that?"

"It's true, I promise. He said the house felt empty without you."

"That's sweet. Do you think I should make the effort and try to contact him?"

"I'm not sure it would do any good. I asked him what he thought about ghosts, and he just laughed."

"That's a shame. Still, as long as he's okay, that's all that matters."

"I asked him if anyone had been trying to sell him jewellery."

"What did he say?"

"They had. In fact, he's already bought some."

"Was it mine?"

"I think so, but you should check for yourself." I took out my phone and showed her the photo.

"Yes, that's definitely my necklace. What's going on, Jill?"

"Someone is stealing jewellery from Ghost Town and then selling it to the surviving relatives back in the human world."

"Who would do something so despicable?"

"I don't know, but I intend to find out."

The guy who had tried to sell Madge's jewellery to her daughter, Cynthia, had left a photograph with his phone number on the back, so after I'd left Lily's, I gave him a call. Much to my surprise, he answered on the first ring.

"Yes?"

"Hi there. My name is Cynthia. You called to see me a little while back and offered to sell me some of my mother's jewellery."

"What about it?"

"I've been giving it more thought, and I might be interested in buying it. Do you still have it?"

"I might. I might not. I thought you weren't interested?"

"I've changed my mind."

"It may be too late now."

"Don't mess me around. Do you have the jewellery or not?"

"As it happens, I do, but the price has gone up."

"That's ridiculous. It was already too expensive."

"Please yourself. Do you want it or not?"

"How much?"

"Three hundred."

"That's daylight robbery."

"Please yourself."

"Wait! I'll need to see it first, to make sure it's the real thing."

"That can be arranged, but it'll have to be at a place of my choosing."

"Can't you just bring it to the house?"

"No. For all I know, you could have tipped off the police. This could be a trap."

"Okay, where do you want to meet?"

"I'll give you a call later this afternoon, to tell you where and when, but I'll warn you now, if you don't show up on time, there'll be no second chance."

"What's your name?"

"You don't need to know that." And with that, he hung up.

***

I had intended to go to Cuppy C yesterday to find out how the twins had fared on their weekend at the country park hotel, but I didn't get the chance, so I decided to check in on them today.

It was quiet in the tea room; Amber was by herself behind the counter. She seemed to be hobbling a little, and kept wincing, as though she was in some kind of discomfort.

"Are you okay, Amber?"

"Yeah, just about."

"You don't look it."

"To tell you the truth, I ache all over."

"After your relaxing weekend at the country park, I expected you to be full of beans."

"Yeah, well, things didn't exactly work out like we expected them to."

"How come?"

"It turned out that we'd actually won an outward-bound weekend held at the country park. We had to do assault courses, and they had us abseiling down rockfaces."

"Oh dear."

"We had to run a cross country too. It was pouring with

rain all the way around, and some of the fields were knee-deep in mud."

I laughed.

"It's not funny, Jill."

"Sorry."

"Pearl is in an even worse state than me."

I laughed even more.

"Jill!"

"Sorry, but you two did kind of ask for it. You were both quick enough to make fun of me when I had my lottery mishap."

"What can I get you, anyway?"

"Just a coffee, please. I can't stay long. How's Aunt Lucy? The last time I saw her she wasn't talking to Lester."

"She still isn't. I assume you heard about his latest job fiasco."

"The dragon slayer? Yeah, I did. I just can't imagine Lester fighting dragons."

"Neither can I, but the more Mum tries to talk him out of it, the more determined he seems to be to go through with it."

***

I'd just finished my coffee when my phone rang. I could tell by the caller ID that it was my friend, the jewellery peddler.

"Be in Washbridge Park by the water fountain in ten minutes."

"I'm not sure I can get there that quickly."

"If you're not there on time, don't bother to contact me

again."

"Okay. I'll get there somehow. How will I know you?"

"Don't worry about that. I'll come to you."

I used the 'doppelgänger' spell to make myself look like Madge's daughter, Cynthia, then magicked myself over to the park where I waited next to the water fountain as instructed. I'd only been there for a couple of minutes when I spotted a figure in the distance. The man was dressed in a long black coat with the hood pulled over his head. He couldn't have looked any more suspicious if he'd been carrying a large banner that read:

I'm a con man

"Have you got the money?" he demanded.

"I want to see the jewellery first."

He reached into his pocket and pulled it out. "Where's the money?"

As soon as we'd made the exchange, he hurried off the same way as he'd come. I immediately made myself invisible and followed him. Ten minutes later, he stopped outside a terraced house. While he was fumbling for his key, I hurried over, to stand by his side, so that I could sneak into the house with him.

Now all I had to do was to bide my time until he left again.

Fortunately, I didn't have too long to wait because less than half an hour later, he put on his coat and went out. Alone in the house now, I searched each room in turn, and eventually struck gold in the back bedroom, where I found a box full of jewellery. This was a bigger operation than I'd imagined. After taking photographs of each of the pieces, I let myself out of the house.

For this scam to work, my friend had to have a partner-in-crime in Ghost Town. Someone to supply him with the jewellery and furnish him with the contact details for the next-of-kin in the human world. To find out who that was, I'd need to wait around until the ghost made contact. I simply didn't have time to do that, but I knew someone who could.

I gave Edna, the surveillance fairy, a call.

"Hello stranger," she said. "I was beginning to think you didn't need my services anymore."

"I've not had any suitable jobs, but something's just cropped up that's right up your street. That's if you're free, of course."

"As luck would have it, I am. What do you need, Jill?"

"I want you to follow someone." I gave her the guy's address and explained the scam that he was running.

"He sounds like a nasty piece of work."

"He is, trust me."

"Let me make sure I've got this right. You want me to keep an eye on him until he's contacted by a ghost."

"That's right. Can you see ghosts, Edna?"

"Of course I can't, but I can tell if someone is talking to one. I'll give you a call the moment the ghost makes contact."

"That's great. Thanks."

"My usual rates will apply, of course."

"Custard creams?"

"What else?"

***

"Where is he?" Kathy greeted me at the door. She barely

looked at me because she was too busy looking over my shoulder. "He is coming, isn't he?"

"Yes, Kathy, Martin is coming, but he's making his own way here. He should be here in the next few minutes."

There was no sign of the kids inside.

"Have Lizzie and Mikey gone to Peter's parents?"

"No. They couldn't take them, unfortunately. The kids are both upstairs in their bedrooms."

"It's unusual for Lizzie not to come and say hello to me."

"She's been in a weird mood recently. I don't know what's got into her. She's much quieter than usual, and she even snapped at me, which isn't like her at all. I guess she's just growing up. I've got used to that kind of thing from Mikey; I suppose I'll have to get used to it from Lizzie too."

"Shall I go upstairs and say hello to her?"

"To be honest, Jill, I'd leave her for now. She was reading when I came downstairs. Why don't you let her come down in her own time?"

"Okay."

Five minutes later, Martin arrived, and I made the introductions. "Martin, this is my sister, Kathy. Kathy, this is my brother, Martin."

"I'm very pleased to meet you, Kathy." He offered his hand, but she ignored it and went in for a hug.

After a few moments, she stepped back. "I can't get over it. You two are so alike."

"It's crazy, isn't it?" Martin said. "I've been trying to work out what this makes you and me, Kathy. I mean, Jill's my sister and you're also her sister. Does that mean we're kind of like sister and brother?"

"We definitely are, bro." Kathy grinned. "Let's go through to the lounge. I've put out a few snacks."

Snacks? A few? I was ravenous.

"Is that all?" I sighed.

"Yeah, just nibbles and things. I assumed you would both have eaten."

"That's fine," Martin said. "I had a big meal less than an hour ago."

Bully for him. I hadn't eaten since lunchtime.

The three of us chatted for just over an hour, but to be honest, it was Kathy and Martin who did most of the talking. I was far too hungry to focus.

It was obvious that Kathy was smitten by Martin. He certainly knew how to ingratiate himself with people. I suppose I should've been pleased that he got on so well with my sister, but I still wasn't sure about him.

I'd just finished the last of the nibbles when Mikey came downstairs.

"Mum, Lizzie is scaring me again."

Kathy took his hand. "This is Martin. He's your uncle."

"But I already have an uncle. Uncle Jack."

"I know you do, but Martin is another uncle. Say hello to him."

"Hello," Mikey managed, rather half-heartedly.

"What do you like to do, Mikey?" Martin asked.

"I like fishing and I want to go go-carting, but Mum won't let me."

Just then, there were more footsteps on the stairs. Moments later, Lizzie came through the door.

"Just look at this little angel, Mikey," Kathy said. "How can you possibly be scared of her?"

"Hi, Lizzie," I said. "How are you?"

"I'm okay, thank you, Auntie Jill." Her voice was flat, and she showed none of her usual sparkle.

"Come on. It's time for you two to go to sleep." Kathy took them both by the hand and led them upstairs.

No sooner had she come back down, than Martin said, "I'm really sorry, Kathy, but I've just remembered something important that I have to do." He stood up and turned to me. "Jill, I came in a taxi. I don't suppose you could give me a lift, could you?"

"Err, sure."

"Thanks again, Kathy." He gave her a hug and kissed her on both cheeks. "We must do this again."

"Are you sure you can't stay any longer?"

"I really can't. This is very important."

Once we were in my car, I confronted him. "What on earth was that all about, Martin? You were quite rude in there."

"I'm sorry, but didn't you see it?"

"See what?"

"The aura."

"I have no idea what you're talking about."

"Lizzie. You must have seen it all around her."

"I didn't see anything."

"I did, and I've seen the same thing before. It's bad news, trust me. Has anything unusual happened to her recently?"

"Not really. Well, she went missing for a short time recently, but she soon turned up again. She'd been following a cat."

"Are you sure that's what she'd been doing?"

"That's what she said."

"Has anything else unusual happened?"

"Mikey's been having a few nightmares. He said that Lizzie came into his room and her eyes were glowing orange, but like I said, that was just a bad dream."

"Anything else? Anything at all, Jill. This is important."

"There are a number of ghosts who live in the house. They mentioned something about Redgrave."

The colour drained from his face. "Oh no."

"What is it, Martin? Do you know this Redgrave person?"

"Red grave isn't a person."

"What is it, then?"

"There's no time to explain. It needs to be stopped or Lizzie will die."

"Stopped? Stop what? Where is it?"

"In Candlefield."

"Let's get over there, then."

"Not in *your* Candlefield. It's in *my* Candlefield. I have to deal with this, but it might take a day or two."

"There's no way I'm staying here while you—"

Before I could finish the sentence, he'd disappeared.

Chapter 18

"You have to let it go, Jill," Jack said over breakfast.

"Let it go?" I almost spat my corn flakes all over him. "And how am I supposed to *let it go*, pray tell? My niece has just apparently been under the control of some kind of weird red thing, and you're telling me to *let it go*?"

"Sorry, I can understand why you're upset."

"I'm *way* beyond upset. I'm mad as hell at Martin."

"What exactly did he say?"

"Not much. He delivered the bombshell about Lizzie, said he'd sort it out, and then disappeared."

"Maybe it's better that you let him handle it. I mean, you've never been to this Candlefield of his."

"I'm not even sure I believe this alternative Candlefield exists. He could be lying. And if he is, what else is he lying about? Just wait until I get my hands on him; he'll wish he'd never found his sister."

"What exactly did he tell you about this red thingy?"

"Nothing, just that it was bad news, and that he had to stop it, or Lizzie could die."

"Does Kathy have any idea what's going on?"

"No, thank goodness. She mentioned that Lizzie had been quiet and that she'd snapped at her, but she just put it down to the fact that she's getting older."

"So, what are you planning on doing?"

"There's nothing I can do. I can't get hold of Martin, and I have no idea how to get to *his* Candlefield. I'm just going to have to wait until I hear from him. Can we talk about something else? Did you talk to Roy?"

"No. I'd intended to, but I lost my nerve. I just wasn't sure how to approach it. Maybe it would be better to see if it blows over."

"You're probably right. By the way, how come you never mentioned how the bowling went last night? I take it you lost?"

"It was a close match."

"So, you did lose?"

"Yeah, but it was really close."

"But you still lost."

"Only because Peter is so jammy. It was all down to his very last shot; he slipped on the approach and ended up getting a strike. I couldn't believe it."

"Just so I'm absolutely clear, you lost?"

"Yes, Jill, I lost, but I'm still up on games overall. By the way, when I came home last night, I saw Mr Ivers and he was acting really weird."

"You say that like it's unusual."

"But this was weird even by his standards. He had his face pressed up against the glass in the toll booth. I've never seen anything like it."

"Actually, there's a reason for that. Do you remember that trinket box I had?"

"The one that Big was in?"

"I gave it to Mr Ivers as a present."

"How come?"

"I thought it might cheer him up. I warned him that under no circumstances must he open the lid, but—"

"Are you telling me that Big was in the toll booth with him?"

"Yeah. That's why Mr Ivers was squashed up against the glass. There's barely enough room in there for him and the big guy."

"I wonder what Big makes of him?"

"He's probably regretting denying me my wishes. The weird thing is, I can still see Big; I have no idea why that is."

"Did he see you?"

"I'm not sure. If he did, he's blanking me. But Mr Ivers is happy now he has a friend."

"It's all rather sad, don't you think?"

"Yeah, but then Mr Ivers is rather sad. Oh yes, while I remember, the dinner with Luther and Rebecca is cancelled."

"How come?"

"She came to see me at the office. It turns out it's a full moon on Friday."

"Cripes. That could have been nasty."

"Very. I've told her I'll tell Luther something's cropped up, and that we'll need to reschedule."

***

When I came out of the house, Britt and Kit were just getting into their car.

"Hi, you two." I waved. "Pity about the marathon. And after you'd trained so hard for it too." Snigger.

"We can't figure it out," Kit said. "We were going great guns; we thought we were going to put in a personal best, but then we hit a brick wall."

"I guess father time catches up with us all eventually."

On my way to work, I called at the corner shop because I needed to buy several packets of custard creams.

What? No, they weren't all for me. They were to pay Edna. Sheesh, just how greedy do you think I am?

Custard creams in hand, I made my way to the counter where little Jack, on stilts as always, was behind the glass screen.

"Hi, Jill."

I was quite surprised to hear his voice because, recently, we'd only been able to communicate via the intercom.

"How come I can hear you, Jack?"

"The intercom was just too much trouble, so, I've had a speaker system installed, which means we can now speak to each other normally."

"That's much better. By the way, Jack, I've been meaning to ask you for a while now, how come you no longer treat me to your thought for the day?"

"The truth is, Jill, I woke up one morning and the well of profoundness was dry."

"That's really sad. Life's just not the same without them."

"I know. I feel the same. Maybe they'll return to me one day."

Just then, the door opened, and a woman came pogoing in. And no, she wasn't a punk rocker; she was on a pogo stick!

To give her her due, she displayed a remarkably high level of control, and she didn't knock anything off the shelves, as she made her way around the aisles.

With a jar of gherkins in her hand (and, yes, she was now holding onto the pogo stick with just one hand), she came over to the counter, handed Jack her money and then pogoed out of the shop.

Little Jack seemed totally unfazed by this strange interlude.

"You did see that, didn't you, Jack? She was on a pogo

stick."

"That's Janice. She often calls in."

"And is she always on the pogo stick?"

"Yes, she goes everywhere on it. Apparently, she won several competitions in her youth. She's always bemoaning the fact that it isn't an Olympic sport."

"Doesn't the pogoing cause problems in the shop?"

"Not since we reached an agreement that she'd avoid the busy periods." He glanced at the biscuits in my arms and did a double take. "How many packets have you got there, Jill?"

"Just the ten."

***

I was just about to go into my office building when I spotted something across the road: A new CCTV camera had been installed on the building directly opposite, so I popped across the road and asked at reception if I could speak to the head of security.

A couple of minutes later, a man wearing a grey uniform, and holding what smelled like a bacon cob, appeared in reception. What a delicious smell. The bacon cob, not the man.

"How can I help you, madam?"

I couldn't stop myself staring at his sandwich.

"I don't officially start for another ten minutes," he said, by way of explanation. "This is my breakfast."

"Don't give it a second thought. Breakfast is the most important meal of the day. The reason I'm here is that I have an office in the building directly opposite."

"Is that the one without the sign?"

"Yes, that's the one. I noticed that you've got a new CCTV camera out front."

"That's right. We added a number of them a couple of weeks back."

"I realise this is a bit cheeky, but we've had a problem with someone defacing property in the common area. Is there any chance I might be able to take a quick look at your CCTV footage, to see if I can spot who was responsible?"

"I don't see why not. Follow me." He led the way to a small office, which had a bank of monitors. "What day did it happen?"

"Sometime on Monday."

"Okay, let's start there." He pulled up the recording for that day and set it on fast forward.

On-screen, I watched dozens of people walk by the entrance to my building. Occasionally, I'd see a face I recognised: Mrs V, Jimmy and Kimmy. But, then, just after eleven-thirty, according to the timestamp, I spotted someone else that I recognised.

Bingo!

The security man made a copy of the relevant section of footage, and sent it to my phone.

"Thanks for that, err — sorry, I don't know your name."

"Roger. Roger Bacon."

Back at my building, I went down the corridor to the offices of Clown.

There was no sign of Kimmy, but Jimmy was on reception — sans costume.

"Hi, Breezy."

"It's Jimmy when I'm not in costume."

"Whatever. I have something to show you."

"I'm sorry, Jill, but I thought we'd made our position perfectly clear. We have nothing further to say until we see you in court."

"Just watch this." I took out my phone and played him the CCTV clip.

"That's PomPom." Jimmy stared at the screen.

Feeling pleased with myself and totally vindicated, I made my way down the corridor to my offices where I found Mrs V wearing a hat—a different one from the one she'd worn the day before.

"Good morning, Mrs V. I see you're sporting a hat again."

"I thought I'd better. Hattie said she might drop in again today, and you know how she feels about a head without a hat on it."

"She's a bit much, that friend of yours, isn't she?"

"Only when it comes to hats. Otherwise she's a really nice lady."

"I've just been down the corridor to Clown."

"I hope you haven't been falling out with them again."

"No, quite the contrary, in fact. I've just told them who was responsible for defacing their sign."

"Who did it?"

"Do you remember that rival of theirs? The other clown school called Red Nose?"

"Vaguely."

"It was the guy who owns Red Nose. He goes by the name of PomPom."

"How on earth did you find out?"

"It was pure luck on my part. On my way into work this morning, I happened to notice that they'd installed a new CCTV camera on the building directly opposite. Their security guy was kind enough to let me watch the footage, and that's when I spotted PomPom. He still had the marker in his hand when he left the building."

"I hope Jimmy and Kimmy apologised to you."

"They did, but it'll be a long time before I forget the way they treated me over this."

When I went through to my office, Winky was on the sofa reading a newspaper. He didn't even look up.

"And a very good morning to you too, Winky."

He glanced over the top of his paper. "Morning."

"So, are you going to tell me who that new lady friend of yours was? The one who came calling yesterday?"

"That was Tuesday."

"That's such a lovely name. I've often thought that if I ever have a little girl, I might call her Tuesday."

"Tuesday isn't her name. Her name is Elsie. I go out with her on a Tuesday. On a Wednesday, I see Ruby; on Thursday, it's Violet; on Friday, I—."

"You are a despicable human being."

"Hey, who are you calling a human being?"

***

I stayed in the office just long enough to check the morning's post because it was time for my regular stint over at CASS.

Ms Nightowl had asked me to pop in and see her before I took my class, so I magicked myself straight over to the headmistress' office.

"Good morning Jill." Ms Nightowl was watering the pot plant in the corner of the room. It looked dead to me, but it wasn't my place to comment. "I wanted to bring you up to speed vis-a-vis the search for a replacement head."

"Have you found someone?"

"Not yet, but we have made an important decision regarding the criteria we will use to identify the right person for the post. The governors and I have held several meetings on the subject, and we've reached the conclusion that the most important quality the person must possess is the ability to protect the Core."

"What about their teaching qualifications?"

"This may sound a strange thing for me to say, but we consider that of secondary importance. During my tenure as headmistress, I've done very little teaching. In fact, I can't remember the last time I took a class. The head of CASS is more of a figurehead; someone who can lead the other staff."

"I see."

"We must protect the Core at all costs because, as you know, if it was to fall into the wrong hands, it could be catastrophic. Can you understand why we have come to that decision?"

"Of course, particularly after what happened with Maligarth."

"So, the point is, Jill, we've decided we must find someone who has exceptional magical powers."

That's when the penny dropped. Oh goodness, she wanted me to take over as head.

"I'm very flattered, headmistress, truly I am, but I couldn't possibly —"

"Not you, Jill." She laughed. "We're looking for a serious, level-headed individual."

And presumably, that ruled me out.

"Yes, of course. I wish you the best of luck with your search." I checked my watch. "I probably should get going because I want to call in at the staff room before I take my class."

"What will your subject be today, Jill?"

"I thought I'd teach the kids a little about the afterlife."

"That's a very interesting choice of subject. Can I ask why you've chosen that?"

"I suppose it's because I've had a lot of interaction with ghosts recently, and it's something most people have very little understanding of."

"Excellent. If I get the chance, I may sit in on your class. I'd be interested to hear what you have to say."

Great!

Chapter 19

I *had* been feeling quite relaxed about the lesson I had planned for today. That was until Ms Nightowl said she might sit in on the class. Of course, when I say 'planned', I don't mean planned in the conventional sense of the word. The thought process had gone something like this:

What shall I talk about today?
Err, ghosts, maybe.
Yeah, why not?

When I arrived at the classroom, the kids were standing around, talking (or in most cases, shouting) and being generally unruly.

"Hey, you lot. That's quite enough. Get to your seats."

They totally ignored me.

"I've just come from Ms Nightingale's office, and she said that she might sit in on the lesson today. Now, get to your seats."

That announcement had an immediate effect: They all returned to their desks in double-quick time, and the room fell silent.

"Thank you. I don't know why you couldn't have done that the first time I asked."

"What are we going to talk about today, Miss?" Fleabert Junior shouted.

"I thought we'd talk about ghosts."

"There's no such thing." He laughed.

"Well, Fleabert, that's where you're wrong. Ghosts are very real, and they even have their own world called Ghost Town, or GT for short."

"Miss is right," Sally Topps said. "My mum told me all

about Ghost Town."

"Your mum's daft, then," Fleabert scoffed.

"That's enough from you, Fleabert. Anymore and I'll report you to the headmistress when she comes."

"Sorry, Miss, but I still say there's no such thing as ghosts."

"I used to think that too, but I can promise you that they're as real as the people in this classroom. Hence today's lesson."

"What's it like there, Miss?" Destiny Braden asked. "In Ghost Town?"

"It's not much different to Candlefield or the human world."

"How can you possibly know that, Miss?" Lucinda Blade said.

"Because I often go there. In fact, I've been there in the last few days."

"Can just anyone go there, Miss?"

"I'm afraid not. Humans certainly can't, and I seem to be one of only a small number of sups who is able to do it."

"How come you can do it, Miss?"

"I don't know."

"What's the point in learning about it if we can't actually go there, Miss?" Fleabert said.

"Because, although you may not be able to visit GT, ghosts are able to make contact with you."

"How's that work, then?"

"The ghost has to attach itself to you."

Destiny Braden shuddered. "I don't like the sound of that, Miss."

"It's not as bad as it sounds. For a ghost to 'attach' itself to you, you simply have to be receptive to the idea. That will allow the ghost to communicate with you. For example, my husband is able to talk to his mother who died quite recently."

"Your husband's a human, isn't he, Miss?"

"That's right, but it works the same for sups too."

Once I'd managed to persuade the kids that ghosts and Ghost Town were indeed real, we had quite an interesting discussion. By the time the lesson ended, I got the feeling that some of them would continue the conversation with their parents when they went home at the end of term. When the bell rang, and the kids filed out of the classroom, I breathed a sigh of relief, mainly because there'd been no sign of Ms Nightowl.

After stopping off at the staff room for coffee and a biscuit, I magicked myself back to Washbridge. I'd no sooner arrived there, than my phone rang; it was Edna.

"Jill, they're here now."

"The ghost?"

"Yeah. Get yourself over here straight away."

I magicked myself to the jewellery peddler's terraced house, but there was no sign of Edna. Where was that fairy?

I'd no sooner thought that than I almost jumped out of my skin when she landed on my left shoulder.

"What are you waiting for, Jill? They're inside now."

"Do you have to do that? You scared me half to death."

"I'm so sorry. I completely forgot to bring my trumpet with me."

"There's no need for sarcasm. Are you sure he's talking

to a ghost?"

"Let's put it this way, I've been watching him for the last couple of hours and he didn't make a sound, and then a few minutes ago, he suddenly started talking."

"Maybe he's talking to himself?"

"No, he's definitely having a conversation with someone, but I can't see them. Are you going to stand around here all day, asking me questions, or are you going to take a look for yourself?"

"Okay, where is he?"

"Around the back, in the kitchen."

"Right, come on then."

"Hold on. I'm not going anywhere. My job here is done. You asked me to wait until the ghost arrived and that's what I've done."

"Fair enough. I'll do it myself."

"Hang on. What about my payment?"

"The custard creams are back at the office. Can you pop in tomorrow to get them?"

"No, I can't, I'm hungry right now. Can't I just go and help myself to them?"

"I suppose so. They're in the bottom drawer of my desk."

"Which one?"

"I don't know. The left one, probably."

"Okay, I'll go and get them now."

"Hey, Edna, don't take all of them. Some of those are mine."

After she'd left, I made my way to the back of the house, and peered through the kitchen window. Edna was right; my friend, the jewellery peddler, was talking to someone, and it was indeed a ghost. And what's more, I recognised that ghost: It was Selina Mowbray who I'd met at the bridge club. She'd struck me as a nasty piece of work at the time, and it seemed my instincts had proven correct.

I couldn't hear what they were saying, and I was just about to cast the 'listen' spell when Selina disappeared. I figured she must have gone back to Ghost Town, so I magicked myself over there too.

I went straight to the bridge club, which was deserted except for Selina who was busy piling the chairs in the corner of the room. She gave me a puzzled look, and clearly had no idea where she knew me from.

"Hello, can I help you?"

"Hi. We met the other day when I gave Madge a lift."

"Oh yes, I remember now. I'm afraid the bridge club isn't open today."

"That's okay. I'm not here about bridge. I'm not sure if you're aware, but Madge, Lily and possibly other members of the bridge club have had jewellery go missing from their houses recently."

"I think I did hear something about that. I just assumed they'd misplaced it."

"That's always possible, but another possibility is that someone who knew they'd be out of the house—at the bridge club, for example—tipped off the thief who then sneaked into their houses and stole their jewellery."

"I have no idea what you're talking about." Her body language said otherwise.

"For argument's sake, let's say that is what happened," I continued. "What if the stolen jewellery was then taken to the human world and sold to the victims' surviving relatives? Wouldn't that be a fine scam?"

Her legs seemed to go from under her, and she had to

take a seat.

"Have you no conscience, Selina?"

"I have nothing to say to you."

"Who was your accomplice? Who broke into the house and stole the jewellery?"

"I don't know anything about any of this."

"Fair enough." I took out my phone and made a call. "Is that Constance Bowler?"

"Speaking."

"It's Jill Maxwell."

"Hi, Jill. Long time no speak."

"I'm at the bridge club here in Ghost Town, and I wondered if you could pop over? There's a lady here who I think you should talk to regarding a spate of jewellery thefts."

Constance arrived fifteen minutes later. After I'd filled her in, she asked Selina to accompany her to the police station.

"Do you need me to come with you, Constance?" I asked.

"I don't think so. I have a feeling that this lady will tell us all we need to know before the day is over."

My job done, I magicked myself back home.

***

Jack and I were on our way to Mrs V's house for dinner.

"How many more times do I have to promise, Jill? I won't let Armi talk me into taking another cuckoo clock."

"You'd better not because one of those things in the house is one too many. And don't forget what I said about not laughing at their house when you see it."

"What do you take me for? I would never be so inconsiderate."

"Jack, stop it! You promised!"

We'd barely got through the gate at Mrs V's house before Jack had doubled up with laughter. Luckily, there was no sign of Mrs V or Armi.

"I'm sorry." Jack managed through tears of laughter. "I thought I was prepared, but I mean, just look at it."

Just then, the front door opened and Mrs V and Armi appeared.

"Is Jack all right, Jill?" Mrs V said.

"He's fine. He's—err—just tying his shoelaces." It was only then that I realised he was wearing slip-ons.

Fortunately, Jack had managed to compose himself. "I'm fine, Mrs V. Sorry about that."

Still slightly puzzled, Mrs V beckoned us inside. "I'm just putting the finishing touches to dinner. Armi will give you a tour of the house until it's ready."

The house was an absolute delight, and the furniture, which Mrs V had chosen, complimented it perfectly. The only thing that spoiled it was the cuckoo clock in every room. The lounge actually had two of them! I would have gone mad if I'd had to live with those. After we'd seen the rest of the house, we made our way to the dining room where, quite remarkably, there was no cuckoo clock.

Mrs V came through from the kitchen.

"How come there isn't a cuckoo clock in here, Mrs V?" I said.

"I insist on having peace and quiet while I'm eating. I

find the cuckooing spoils my appetite." She checked her watch. "Dinner will only be a few minutes now."

With Mrs V back in the kitchen, Jack made the mistake of asking Armi how he made the cuckoo clocks. I was just wondering what I could stuff into my ears so I wouldn't have to listen, when I happened to glance out of the window, and I spotted William Twigmore, the wood nymph, standing by the treeline. There was no way I was going to allow those horrible creatures to disturb our dinner, so I said I needed some fresh air, and nipped out.

When I got outside, there was no sign of Twigmore.

"William, where are you? Come on out. I know you're there." There was no response and still no sign of him. "William!"

"Jill, what are you doing?" Mrs V was standing in the doorway.

"Err—nothing. Just getting some fresh air."

"It sounded like you were calling to someone called William."

"Err, no. I was just saying—err—that this is a view in a *million*."

"It's just trees."

"Yeah, I adore trees."

She gave me what could only be described as a pitying look. "You'd better come in; dinner is on the table."

"Okay." I took one last look at the treeline, but there was still no sign of the wood nymphs.

Mrs V had made a delicious roast dinner with all the trimmings. Ten minutes in, I heard a noise coming from the kitchen. No one else seemed to notice, but I had a horrible feeling I knew what it was, so I excused myself, supposedly to go to the loo.

I hurried through to the kitchen and, as I suspected, there on the table were the three wood nymphs. They'd opened the biscuit barrel and were helping themselves to the contents.

"Stop that, you three." I launched myself at them, but they were too quick, and I ended up knocking the biscuit barrel onto the floor, spilling out all of the biscuits. Meanwhile, the wood nymphs made their escape through the open window.

"What are you doing, Jill?" I turned around to find Mrs V staring at me in disbelief.

"Err—nothing."

"If you weren't enjoying the dinner, dear, you should've said so."

"I am enjoying it, honestly. I was just looking for—err—tomato sauce."

"On a roast dinner?"

"Oh yes. I love tomato sauce on my roasts."

"Right?" She pulled open one of the cupboards, took out a bottle of ketchup, and handed it to me.

"Thanks. I'll just pick up these biscuits."

"Leave them. Your dinner will go cold. I'll see to that later."

Back in the dining room, I had no choice but to put sauce on my dinner, earning me puzzled looks from Armi and Jack.

Yuk.

***

As we drove home, Jack began to laugh.

"What's amusing you?"

"The tomato sauce."

"What choice did I have? I could hardly tell her the real reason I was in the kitchen."

"How did the dinner taste with tomato sauce on it?"

"Shut up."

As I was getting out of the car, I noticed a box on the back seat.

"What's that, Jack?"

"What?"

"That box on the back seat."

"Oh, that's nothing."

"What's in it?"

"I'm sorry, Jill, but Armi was very persuasive."

Chapter 20

It was the next morning, and we were in the kitchen.

"Jack dearest, would you like me to make you another cup of coffee?"

He eyed me suspiciously. "What are you after, Jill?"

"What makes you think I want something? I'm just asking if you'd like a cup of coffee."

"Come on. Spit it out. You might as well tell me what it is you want."

"Well, there is something, but it's nothing really."

"Hmm. Let's be hearing it."

"It's just that, when I spoke to the partner of one of the men who went missing from a hotel, she told me she'd discovered her husband had transferred a quarter of a million pounds out of one of his bank accounts just a few days before he vanished."

"Oh?" Jack suddenly seemed much more interested. "Are you sure about that?"

"Positive. She showed me the entry on the bank statement. I was just wondering if there's any chance you might be able to track down the account that the money was sent to?"

"Probably not, but if you jot down the account number, I'll see what I can do."

That wasn't the response I'd been expecting; I'd assumed he would say no, right off the bat. Curiosity got the better of me.

"How come you're willing to do this?" I jotted down the number and handed it to him. "You normally tell me to get lost when I ask for help."

"Don't build your hopes up. I can't promise I'll come up

with anything, but I'll see what I can do."

He was definitely up to something, but I couldn't figure out what it was.

***

When I arrived at the office, there was a bunch of flowers on Mrs V's desk.

"Do you have a secret admirer Mrs V?"

"These aren't for me, Jill. They're for you."

She handed them to me, and I checked the card. "Our sincere apologies. Jimmy and Kimmy (AKA Breezy and Sneezy)."

"That's nice of them, isn't it dear? Will you forgive them now?"

"I suppose so. We all make mistakes, but I might let them sweat for a little while longer. I think they deserve that much."

I was just about to go through to my office when Mrs V said, "Hattie came in earlier."

"Wow, she's an early bird."

"She brought a selection of hats for you to try."

"She never gives up, does she?"

"I've taken them through to your office."

Winky was on my desk, surrounded by hats of all shapes, sizes and colours.

"What do you think of this one?" He was wearing a little green number with a flower on top.

"I think you look totally ridiculous."

"How about this one, then?"

"Still ridiculous, and get off my desk, will you? Those

hats aren't for you."

He jumped down, hurried across the room, and jumped onto the sofa. "Go on then," he said. "Let's see you try them on."

"I don't suit a hat."

"Go on, what do you have to lose? Live a little."

"Okay then." I picked up a yellow one. "What do you think of this?"

"Nah, that's not you."

"How about this one?"

"Too big. You look ridiculous."

Twelve hats later: "That's the one," he said.

"Are you sure?"

"Yeah, that one is definitely you."

"I don't have a mirror to look at myself."

He jumped back onto my desk. "Give me your phone."

I did as he said, and he snapped a photo of me and handed the phone back.

"I do look good in this, don't I? I might keep this one."

"Good for you. By the way, that psycho fairy was in here yesterday, rummaging through your drawers."

"Edna? Yeah, I told her she could get the custard creams that I owed her."

"She took the lot. Cleared out the drawer."

"She did what?" I checked my desk, and he was right. "What a liberty!"

***

Alison Robbins' husband, Charlie, had also vanished from a hotel. His disappearing act had taken place just over a year ago, from a hotel in Cromer. Alison lived in

Mansfield, and she'd agreed that I could pay her a visit, but first I needed a coffee, so I called in at Coffee Games.

I'd no sooner walked through the door of the coffee shop than someone handed me a parcel. This was turning out to be my lucky day: First a bunch of flowers and now a present. I was just about to rip it open when someone grabbed my arm.

"Hey, what do you think you're doing?" he said.

"Sorry?"

"You can't unwrap the parcel."

"Why not? Someone just gave it to me."

"Yes, but the music hasn't stopped yet. Duh!"

That's when I realised that I'd walked in on a game of pass the parcel.

"Oh, right. Sorry." I handed it to the person nearest to me and then made my way to the counter where Piers was on duty.

"Morning, Piers."

"Good morning, Jill. Your usual caramel latte and a muffin?"

"Yes, please. How's business?"

"A bit quiet today. Pass the parcel isn't one of our more popular games."

Once I had my drink and cake, I headed towards a window table, but before I could take a seat, someone called my name. To my dismay, it was Mr Ivers who was sharing his booth with my green chum, Big.

"Won't you come and join me, Jill?" Mr Ivers beckoned me over.

"I'd love to," I said, through gritted teeth.

There was barely enough space for me to squeeze in

next to Mr Ivers because Big was taking up all the room.

"Could you budge up a little, Mr Ivers?" I said, knowing full well that he couldn't.

"I'm sorry, Jill, the seat next to me is a little damp," he lied.

Big glanced over at me, but he still showed no sign of recognition.

"Is it your day off, Mr Ivers?"

"It is indeed. I thought I'd grab a quick coffee, then Big and I will—err—I mean I'll do some work on the next newsletter."

"Sorry, did you just say you and *Big*?"

"Err, no. It's just me. No one else. I don't know anyone called Big."

Sure, you don't. Snigger.

After a couple of minutes, Mr Ivers excused himself and went to the loo, leaving Big and me by ourselves.

"Hey, big guy. How's it hanging?"

"Are you talking to me?"

"Don't you remember me?"

"I don't think so. Should I?"

"You were with me just a few days ago. I let you out of the trinket box."

"That would explain it. Once I've had a sleep in the box, my memory is wiped clean, so I wouldn't remember you. How long was I with you?"

"Quite a while."

"Did we have a good time together?"

"Yes, I would say so."

"Why did I end up back in the trinket box?"

"You said you were missing it, so I let you go back."

"I see."

"How are you getting on with Mr Ivers?"

"To tell you the truth, he's a bit boring. All he ever talks about is movies and hand puppets. I might sneak back into the trinket box when he's not looking."

"Have you granted him any wishes?"

"Of course not. It's too much hassle. Did I grant you any?"

"No, you didn't."

"It's probably for the best. People always waste them."

What kind of excuse was that? Who in their right mind would squander three perfectly good wishes?

After Mr Ivers and Big had left, I took one bite of the muffin, but I couldn't face anymore because I was feeling a little queasy. What a waste.

I couldn't stop worrying about Lizzie. Needless to say, I'd heard nothing from Martin, so I decided to pop down to Kathy's shop, to see if I could find out how she was doing.

There was no one in the shop except for Kathy who looked surprised to see me.

"What brings you down here? Let me guess. You're after a free drink."

"Actually no. I've just been to Coffee Games, but thanks, anyway."

"I probably shouldn't tell you this, Jill, but I've got a new packet of custard creams in the back."

"I'm okay, thanks."

"Are you feeling all right? I've never known you to turn down a custard cream before."

"I've just had a muffin and I'm quite full," I lied.

"If you aren't here to scrounge a drink, why *are* you

here?"

I didn't want to alarm Kathy by letting her see that I was worried about Lizzie, so I would have to be very subtle.

"Is Lizzie okay?" I blurted out. "I'm really worried about her."

What do you mean that wasn't very subtle?

"Lizzie? Yeah, she's fine."

"Are you sure? I thought she seemed a bit off it when Jack and I came over the other day."

"She was out of sorts for a couple of days, but when she got up this morning, she was as bright as a button."

"You're not just saying that?"

"Of course not. She was bouncing around the house as normal this morning before she went to school."

"That's great. Anyway, I can't stop, I have to go to Mansfield on a case I'm working on."

"Okay, catch you later."

I had planned to drive to Mansfield, but I was still feeling a little queasy, so I thought I'd save myself the bother and magicked myself there instead. Alison Robbins' husband, Charlie, had disappeared from a hotel in Cromer, just over a year ago. As far as I could make out, the circumstances were very similar to Eddie Broom's case, but I wanted to hear it directly from Alison.

She must have seen me walking up the drive because the door was open before I had the chance to knock.

"Hi, I'm Jill Maxwell. I called you yesterday."

"Please come in. I was quite surprised to get your call. It's a while now since anyone's mentioned Charlie. Would you like a drink?"

"Not for me, thanks."

"Let's go through to the living room. We can talk in there."

As soon as I walked into the room, I noticed several photographs on the sideboard, of Alison and a man with greying brown hair.

"Is that Charlie?"

"No, that's Rupert, who I'm with now."

"I see."

"The truth is, Mrs Maxwell — "

"Please call me Jill."

"The truth is, Jill, Charlie and I had started to drift apart long before he vanished. It would have been only a matter of time before the marriage had ended, even if he hadn't disappeared. Rupert and I have been seeing each other for the best part of three months now. He's so very different from Charlie. So giving, so caring."

"I see."

"What exactly did you want to ask me?"

"I've read the newspaper reports, but I'd like to hear your version of what happened."

"I'm sure you're already aware that Charlie disappeared from a hotel."

"Yes, that's what drew me to this case, actually. Don't you find it strange that he was staying in a budget hotel?"

"More than strange. The idea of staying in a budget hotel would have brought him out in hives."

"What exactly was he doing in Cromer?"

"He'd gone there for a couple of days, on business, supposedly."

"Why do you say *supposedly*?"

"Two reasons: I'd never known him mention any

business in Cromer, and to be honest, I was pretty sure he was seeing other women."

"You were telling me what happened at the hotel."

"When he didn't come home, I contacted them. They told me they hadn't seen him since the day he'd booked in. It was all very strange."

"What did the police have to say?"

"I got the impression they thought he'd disappeared deliberately. And to be honest, I think there's a good chance that they're right."

"If there were problems with the marriage, why didn't he just ask for a divorce?"

"Money. Plain and simple."

"Has his disappearance left you in difficulties? Moneywise?"

"Not really. Charlie and I had a substantial amount of money held in joint accounts, which I have now moved to my individual account."

"Do you think he had more money squirrelled away?"

"I'm absolutely sure of it. In numerous accounts probably. Wait there for a minute, would you?" She left the room and returned a couple of minutes later. "Look at this." She showed me a bank statement. "The slime ball transferred a quarter of a million out of our joint accounts a few days before he did a runner."

"Do you have any idea where the money went to?"

"None, but I'm pretty sure he must have sent it to some sort of offshore account."

I glanced at the account number on the statement; I'd seen that same number before.

Chapter 21

Margaret Bowler and Allison Robbins had both shown me evidence that their husbands had transferred a quarter of a million pounds out of their bank accounts, just days before they'd disappeared. In both cases, the money had been transferred to the same unknown account.

It was just about possible that the budget hotel connection was a coincidence, but there was no way that these identical quarter of a million pound transfers could be. The curious thing was that neither Lorraine Cross nor Sandra Broom had mentioned a similar transfer of funds in relation to Eddie's disappearance. Surely, if that had happened, one of them would have told me; it wasn't exactly the kind of thing that would slip your mind.

I gave Lorraine a call first.

"Lorraine, it's Jill."

"Do you have any news for me?"

"Nothing yet, sorry. Look, this may sound like a strange question, but do you know if Eddie transferred a large sum of money out of one of his bank accounts, just prior to his disappearance?"

"No, but then I'd only know if he'd told me about it. Sandra would know for sure. Have you asked her?"

"Not yet, but I intend to."

"What kind of money are we talking about?"

"A quarter of a million pounds."

"*A quarter of a million*?" She laughed. "No way. Sandra and Eddie were quite well off, but they didn't have that kind of money. Why do you ask, anyway?"

"It's probably nothing. I'll keep you posted, Lorraine."

I rang Sandra next.

"I have nothing else to say to you. I've already answered your questions. I'd rather just forget all about the matter."

I could hardly believe the callousness of the woman, dismissing her husband's disappearance as a *matter*.

"Sandra, please, this will only take a minute."

"It had better."

"Is there any chance that Edward could have transferred a large sum of money out of one of his bank accounts, just prior to his disappearance?"

"I can't say for certain because, as I mentioned before, I'm pretty sure he had bank accounts that I knew nothing about, but I didn't see any unusual transfers. What kind of money are we talking about?"

"A quarter of a million pounds."

Just like Lorraine, Sandra laughed. "No chance. Edward might have had a bit of cash squirrelled away, but he certainly didn't have that kind of money."

"Okay, Sandra, thanks for your time."

***

When I arrived back at the building, Mrs V was in my office.

"Hattie phoned a few minutes ago, Jill. She wanted to know if you liked any of the hats."

I went over to my desk and picked up the one I'd tried on earlier. "Yes, I quite like this one, actually."

"Shall I tell Hattie you want to buy it?"

"Why not? It's time I treated myself. Tell her to let me know how much I owe her, will you?"

I'd only been at my desk for a few minutes when a petite, black cat jumped in through the window. Totally ignoring me, she went over to the sofa to join Winky.

"Hello, gorgeous," he said. "I've been looking forward to seeing you all day."

"Hello, Winky, darling."

And then the two of them shared a kiss.

"Hey, you two. Get a room."

The black cat seemed to notice me for the first time. "You didn't tell me that your two-legged could talk to us, Winky."

"I try not to encourage her."

"You must be Thursday," I said.

Winky looked daggers at me.

The black cat looked a little confused. "Thursday? No, my name is Violet."

"My mistake. It's just that Winky told me he was seeing Thursday today. Wait a minute. Now I remember. What he actually said was that he was seeing Violet on Thursday. It's Elsie on Tuesday and Ruby on Wednesday. That's right, isn't it, Winky?"

Violet turned on Winky. "Are you two-timing me?"

"Me? No, I would never do that."

"Who are Elsie and Ruby, then?"

"I have no idea, honestly."

"Who else are you seeing behind my back, Winky?"

"No one, I promise. It's just you, Violet."

"Then why did your two-legged just say you'd referred to me as Thursday?"

"You don't want to take any notice of anything she says. She doesn't know what she's talking about half the time. Only a couple of days ago, she was talking to an imaginary green giant."

"That's not true, Winky," I said. "You told me you had a different lady friend for every day of the week."

Violet swiped him across the face with her paw. "You're a lowlife slime ball. "I don't ever want to see you again." And with that, she jumped off the sofa and headed straight out of the window.

"Oh dear," I said. "She seemed a little upset."

"How could you do that?" He raged. "I had a table booked and everything."

"That'll teach you to treat your lady friends so badly."

"I'll get you back for this. You see if I don't."

"Talk to the hat because the hand isn't listening."

Five minutes later, my phone rang. At first, I didn't think there was anyone there, and that it was one of those annoying automated calls. I was just about to hang up when I heard a soft voice.

"Jill, is that you? Are you there?"

"Who's that? Can you speak up? You're very quiet."

"It's me, Lester."

"Oh? Hi, Lester. The signal isn't very good; I can barely hear you."

"I daren't speak any louder in case the dragon hears me."

"*Dragon*? Where are you?"

"I'm in a cave somewhere in the Black Woods. The dragon is just outside. I don't know what to do."

"Can't you just magic yourself away from there?"

"I've tried that, but for some reason my magic won't work here. I didn't know what to do. That's why I called you. Will you help?"

"Of course. Stay put. I'll be straight over."

It took all of my focus to lock in on his location, but once I'd managed it, I magicked myself over there, to find Lester cowering at the back of the cave.

"Is that you, Jill?" he said in a hushed voice.

"Yes, it's me. You can come out now. Where's the dragon?"

"Shush." He put his finger to his lips. He's just outside somewhere." Lester stood up and came over to me. "He'll find us any minute now. Can you get us out of here?"

"Take my hand."

I magicked the two of us back to my office, where Lester sank into a chair. "I thought I was a goner there."

"What happened, exactly?"

"It was our first day of training. We were with two instructors, and we'd just reached a clearing in the woods when we heard the dragon's wings. I assumed the instructors would know what to do, but they seemed just as scared as the rest of us. Everyone ran for cover. I kept on running and didn't look back, but then I heard the flapping sound getting closer, so I ducked into the cave. That's when I rang you. I'm really sorry, but I didn't know what else to do."

"Don't be so silly. I'm glad you did."

"I'll be okay in a minute or two."

"I assume this will be the end of your plans to become a dragon slayer?"

"Definitely. I'm never going back there."

"What will you do now? Go back to the grim reapers?"

"I can't. I told them where they could shove their job."

"Oh dear."

"I don't know what I'm going to tell Lucy. She was

against me doing this from the very start. When I tell her that I'm out of work, she's going to be livid."

"As it happens, I know of a job going here in the human world, but it's probably not exactly what you're looking for."

"Right now, Jill, I'll consider anything."

"Okay. Let me make a phone call."

***

It took Lester a while, but he finally regained his composure, and headed back to Candlefield. Aunt Lucy would no doubt be delighted that he'd dropped the idea of becoming a dragon slayer, but I wasn't too sure how she'd react when she learned about his new job.

Meanwhile, for obvious reasons, Winky wasn't talking to me. I didn't care because it meant I'd be able to concentrate on my work.

At least, until I got the most exciting phone call EVER.

"Already?" I said.

"Yes, Mrs Maxwell, you can come and view it whenever you like."

"Does that mean it's already on display for the public to see?"

"No, not yet. That won't happen until the weekend, but you can see it in the viewing room right now. Just call at reception and they'll show you where to go."

"Did you hear that, Winky? My waxwork model is ready."

"Whoop-di-do. I assume it's in the chamber of horrors section?"

"You're only jealous because no one wants to make a

waxwork of you."

"Hey, don't forget you're talking to Washbridge's best dressed cat."

"Yeah, but that's not the same as having your own waxwork, is it?"

Still bubbling with excitement, I magicked myself over to Candlefield Wax Museum.

"Hi there. Someone called to say that my waxwork was ready to view."

"What's your name, please?"

"Jill Maxwell."

"Let me check. Oh yes, that's right. It's in the viewing room, which is down that corridor. Take a left, then a right, then another right and then a left. Got that?"

"Err, I'm sure I'll find it." I shot off down the corridor, and although I got lost a couple of times, I eventually found a door with a sign that read: Viewing Room.

I started to open the door, but then nerves got the better of me, and I hesitated. It's one thing seeing a photograph of yourself, but to see a life-size waxwork model. That was something entirely different.

Eventually, I summoned up the courage to go inside where I found a number of waxworks standing in a row: The first one was an elderly wizard. The second was a young vampire, holding a tennis racket. The third, a fairy, had a pen in her hand. The fourth one was a short, ugly witch holding a broomstick, and the last one was an elderly werewolf. There was no sign of my waxwork anywhere.

Perhaps there was more than one viewing room.

I made my way back to reception.

"Hi, I was here a few minutes ago. I'm supposed to be viewing my waxwork model. My name is Jill Maxwell."

"Yes, it's in the viewing room."

"I've just been down there, but it isn't in there."

"According to my paperwork it should be."

"Is there someone who could check what's happened to it?"

"I'll give Billy a call; he looks after the viewing room. If you go back down there, I'll get him to meet you there."

"Okay."

I'd been outside the door for a couple of minutes when an eager young man came skipping down the corridor.

"Are you Billy?"

"That's me. And you must be Jill."

"That's right."

"I understand you're here to see your waxwork?"

"Yes. I took a look inside, but it wasn't there."

"That's strange. I saw it in there earlier. Let's go take a look."

I followed him into the room, and down the row of waxworks. He stopped in front of the short, ugly witch, holding a broomstick.

"There you are. That's yours."

I stared at it in disbelief. "I don't look anything like that."

"I think they've captured your nose."

"It's not even the same height as me." I stood next to it. "Look, it only comes up to my shoulder."

"I see what you mean; it is a little on the short side. Maybe we could put it on a plinth."

"No, no, no! This is all wrong. Where's the guy who made this? The guy who I saw when I came the first time?

What's his name? Err, it rhymes with waxwork."

"Do you mean Max Kirk?"

"That's him. Go and get him."

"I can't."

"Why not?"

"I'm afraid he's on vacation for a couple of weeks."

"In that case, I suggest you give him a call."

"I'm afraid he's not contactable."

"Whatever you do, you cannot put this thing out on display."

Chapter 22

"Aren't you going to eat that?" Jack was eyeing the sausage that I'd left on my plate.

"No, you can have it if you like."

"It's not like you, not to eat all of your breakfast. Are you okay?"

"I'm fine. I'm just not very hungry this morning."

He took a bite of the sausage. "When did you say that waxwork of yours would be ready?"

"I'm not sure."

"I thought you said that it'd be a couple of weeks, so it should be anytime now."

"I think it's going to take longer than that. More like two months."

"That's a pity. I was looking forward to seeing a photo of it."

I shrugged.

Just then, Jack's phone rang, and I could tell from his end of the conversation that it had something to do with the hotel case. When he'd finished on the call, I asked him what it was all about.

"Fingers crossed. We may have a lead."

"Can't you tell me anything else?"

"Only that it's related to that quarter of a million pound transfer. We may have tracked down the account it was sent to."

"Who does it belong to?"

"I can't tell you that. It hasn't even been confirmed yet."

"Come on, Jack. I was the one who alerted you to the other case where a similar cash transfer had been made."

"Sorry, I can't."

"I gave you my last sausage."

"Only because you didn't want it. If it's confirmed, the best I can do is to check if there was a similar transfer into that account from your guy."

"Thanks. You're my favourite husband." I gave him a kiss. "Even if you do taste like a sausage."

***

Jack left for work before me, and I was just about to get into the car when I heard someone shouting, "Freddy? Where are you, Freddy?"

Norm and Naomi Normal were walking up and down the street, and they both looked distressed. Now, if I'd had any sense, I would have got into the car and driven away.

"Hey, you two, is something wrong?"

"We've lost Freddy," Naomi said.

"Who's Freddy?"

"Our pet ferret. I didn't realise that Naomi had let him out of his cage. I left the door open when I took the rubbish to the bin, and he must have sneaked out."

"I didn't realise you had a ferret."

"We've had Freddy for ages; he's our darling little boy. I don't suppose you've seen him, have you, Jill?"

"No, sorry."

"Please be careful when you drive away, just in case he runs out in front of you."

"Yes, of course."

When I reached the toll bridge, Mr Ivers was looking down in the dumps, and I didn't need to ask why. There was no sign of Big in the toll booth, so I assumed Mr Ivers' constant prattle about movies and hand puppets had driven the big guy back into his box.

"Good morning, Mr Ivers. You're looking a bit glum today."

"You know how it is, Jill. Life sucks."

"Cheer up. It's the weekend tomorrow."

"Another long weekend all alone."

I handed him the cash and drove away. What else could I do? There was nothing I could say that would have made a difference. The guy was a hopeless case.

***

I was on the outskirts of Washbridge when a voice from the back seat almost caused me to crash the car. What on earth was going on? I pulled into the side of the road and looked around, to find a ferret sitting there.

"What are you doing in here?"

"I fancied a ride out. It's boring being stuck in that house all the time."

"I assume you're Freddy?"

"That's me. Where are we going?"

"*I'm* going to work, but you need to go back home."

"Please don't take me back. Those two are so boring. They never do anything."

"That's not my problem."

"If you send me back, I'll only escape again."

"Okay, but if I let you come to work with me, do you promise to let me take you home tonight, and not to run away again?"

"Yeah, I promise. Where are we going?"

"To my office in Washbridge, but I should warn you that I have a cat there."

"Cool, I love cats."

I was undecided if I should call the Normals, to let them know I'd found Freddy. In the end, I decided against it. They'd no doubt want to come and get him, and if they did that, he'd just run away again. Better to let him spend the day with me, and reunite him with the Normals tonight. I would tell them that I'd just found him in the back garden.

I parked the car, and said to Freddy, "Get in this bag and don't make a sound. And, whatever you do, don't show yourself until I give you the word."

"It looks a bit grotty in there."

"Never mind that. Just get in. Otherwise you'll have to stay in this car all day."

Somewhat reluctantly, he climbed into the bag. "It smells of old socks in here."

"No, it doesn't. Keep quiet and don't move. I don't want you to scare Mrs V."

"Who's Mrs V?"

"She works for me and if she sees that I have a ferret in my bag, she'll probably have a heart attack."

"Okay. I'll be quiet."

"And keep still."

"Yes, I promise."

I'd just walked into the office building when who should follow me in but Jimmy and Kimmy.

"Hi, Jill." The two of them were all smiles now.

"Morning."

"Did you get the flowers we sent you?"

"I did. They were very nice."

"And you read our apology?"

"Yes, I did." I had no intention of making this easy for them.

"We should never have said the things we did. We've told our solicitor to drop the case obviously, and you'll be pleased to know that we've decided not to bother with a sign at all."

"Oh?"

"We figured that people will be able to work out where we are. And, like you said, we should have taken your views into consideration."

"Right, thanks."

"Are we good now? Friends again?"

"Yes, of course."

"What was that?" Kimmy glanced at my bag.

"What?"

"I thought I saw something move in your bag."

"You must be mistaken."

"I could've sworn I saw something."

"I'd better get going." I started up the stairs. "Lots to do."

Before going into the office, I warned Freddy, "Don't move a muscle or you'll be sorry."

"I have an itch."

"I don't care. Don't move."

I planned to say a quick hello to Mrs V and then hurry through to my office, but she collared me.

"Jill, I told Hattie that you liked that hat."

"Okay, great."

"She asked me to give you this." She passed me an envelope. "That's the bill for it. Hattie asked if you'd let her have the money within a few days."

"Okay, thanks."

"Are you okay Jill? You seem a bit flustered this morning."

"I'm fine. I just need to make some calls."

Once I was in my office, I said to Freddy, "You can come out of there now."

"Thanks." He stretched. "There wasn't much room in there."

"What's that thing?" Winky was glaring at the ferret.

"This is Freddy."

"Yes, but *what* is he?"

"A ferret."

"Why have you brought a ferret into work?"

"He's only come for the day."

"Hi." Freddy waved to Winky.

"Don't '*hi*' me. This is my domain. You'd better stay over that side of the room or there'll be trouble. And don't even think about coming anywhere near my salmon."

"Stop it, you two, I have enough on my plate today. I don't need any aggro from either of you."

"How much?" I double-checked the bill, thinking I must have misread it.

"What's up with you?" Winky said.

"Do you remember that hat I tried on yesterday?"

"Yeah. What about it?"

"This bill is for one-hundred and fifty pounds. That's insane."

"I should go into the millinery business." Winky grinned. "I could make a killing."

"Why would I pay that kind of money for a hat that I'll

probably only ever wear once?"

"You could wear it at your desk. It would be a talking point. People would say, 'Why is that nutter wearing a hat at her desk'."

Before I could give Winky a piece of my mind, Mrs V came through the door. It was only my quick thinking—grabbing Freddy and dropping him into the bottom drawer of my desk—that prevented her from seeing him.

"Have you seen how much your friend, Hattie, wants to charge me for this hat?"

"Hattie's hats don't come cheap, dear. I should've warned you about that."

"It's daylight robbery."

"I have Amber and Pearl out here. They wondered if you could spare them a few minutes."

It was very unusual for the twins to pop in unannounced. Who was running the tea room, I wondered?

"Just give me a minute, then send them through, would you?"

As soon as Mrs V was out of the door, I opened the drawer.

"Why did you put me in here?" Freddy popped his head out. "It's dark and it smells even worse than your bag."

"Sorry, you can come out now."

"Why have you got a weasel in your office, Jill?" Amber said.

"It's not a weasel; it's a ferret."

"Okay." Pearl rolled her eyes. "Why do you have a *ferret* in your office?"

"He's only here for a day."

"But why is he here at all?"

"He's doing work experience. Does it really matter?"

"There's no need to snap," Amber said. "We only popped in to say hello."

"Sorry, girls. I'm having a really bad day. Would you like a drink?"

"No thanks," Pearl said. "We're not stopping. We came over to do a little shopping, and we thought we'd see if you wanted to join us."

"Thanks, but I'm snowed under at the moment. Who's looking after Cuppy C?"

"Mum's got the little ones and the guys are running the shop."

"Will they be okay?"

"Probably not. We'll just have to pick up the pieces tomorrow."

"How's Aunt Lucy?"

"She's a lot happier since Lester abandoned the idea of becoming a dragon slayer."

"Has he? I had no idea."

"Yeah. Apparently, he found the work too boring."

"That's what he told your mum, is it?"

"Yeah. He said it was tedious."

"What's he going to do now?"

"We don't know. He reckons he's got another job, but he's being very secretive about it. He won't even tell Mum what it is."

"That sounds a bit fishy. Still, it can't be any worse than being a grim reaper or a dragon slayer."

"Hey, Jill," Amber said. "When is that waxwork of yours going to be ready?"

"It'll be ages yet. Probably six months or so."

"I'm sure you said it would be a couple of weeks."

"You must have misheard. Six months at the very least. Maybe even a year."

"We can't wait to see it, can we, Pearl?"

"No. We've told everyone who comes into the shop about it. As soon as it's on display, they'll all be there to see it."

"That's great, but like I said, it'll be ages yet. They might even decide not to bother making it. I've heard they sometimes change their minds."

***

Not long after the twins had left, I received a phone call from Constance Bowler over in Ghost Town.

"Jill, do you have a minute for a quick chat about Selena Mowbray?"

"Sure. I'll pop over to the police station now, shall I?"

"Would you meet me in Cakey C instead?"

"Okay, I'll be with you in a couple of minutes."

"Shall I get you a drink and something to eat?"

"Just a coffee for me, please. A caramel latte."

I turned to Winky and Freddy. "While I'm gone, there's to be no funny business from you two."

"I can't help being funny," Winky said. "It just comes naturally to me."

"You know what I mean. Stay in that half of the room. And, Freddy, you stay in your half."

"That's fine by me," Freddy said. "I enjoy looking out of this window. There's lots of stuff happening out there. Do you think I could stay here for another day?"

"No, you can't. You have to go back home."

"But it's really boring there. Will you let me come with you again next week?"

"Okay, but only if you behave yourself while you're with the Normals."

"I will. I promise."

"And when I get back, I expect this office to look just like it does now."

"Like a tip, you mean?" Winky said.

Ignoring his snide remark, I magicked myself over to Cakey C where Constance had a drink waiting for me.

"Thanks for popping over, Jill. I hope you don't mind meeting me here, but I was out and about anyway, and I was gasping for a coffee."

"No problem."

"I just wanted to bring you up to speed with what happened yesterday."

"Did Selena Mowbray confess?"

"She did. Not only that, she also gave up her accomplice."

"Who was it?"

"Her *gentleman* friend."

"Is he some kind of cat burglar?"

"No, but then he didn't need to be. Selena lifted the house keys from the coats and bags of the women while they were playing bridge, then passed them to her accomplice. He let himself into the houses, took whatever jewellery he could find, along with details of their loved ones who were still alive. He always returned the keys before the end of the bridge session, so no one was any the wiser. They might have got away with it too if it hadn't been for Madge being so observant. We're now in the process of trying to identify who all the jewellery that was recovered belongs to."

"That sounds like a result."

"Definitely, and we have you to thank for that."

Chapter 23

Constance had taken a phone call from the station, and she'd had to rush off. I was just finishing my coffee when Yvonne came from behind the counter to join me.

"Do you have a minute, Jill?"

"Yes, of course. Is everything okay?"

"Fine, yeah. Roy and I had a really long talk last night."

"How did it go?"

"Not very well at first, to be perfectly honest. In fact, we had a blazing row."

"Oh dear."

"He asked me again why I was working here, and if I was seeing anyone. I took it for so long, but then I saw red, and I let him have both barrels. We were shouting at one another for the best part of five minutes, but eventually, after we both realised how stupid we were being, we calmed down. We're really lucky that we're able to have contact with one another; so many couples in our position don't. And as Roy pointed out, we never used to argue like that when I was alive, so it's ridiculous to do it now."

"How did you leave things?"

"I'm sure he still doesn't like the idea of me working, but he's accepted that it's something I need to do. Something I want to do."

"What about the other issue?"

"That's much more difficult. It's a weird position that we find ourselves in. Ideally, we'd like to be together, and maybe in time we will be, but for now, we both have to be free to live our own lives."

"And does Roy see it that way?"

"I think so. It's not been easy for either of us."

"But you'll keep in touch?"

"Of course we will. Although the conversation was quite fraught at times, it ended on a happy note."

"That's great to hear. Jack will be delighted."

"That's really why I wanted to talk to you, Jill. I figured you would probably have told Jack about our problems."

"I — err —"

"It's okay, but will you tell him there's no need to worry about us? We're okay now, honestly."

"Of course I will. I'll tell him tonight."

***

I was a little nervous about what might be waiting for me back at the office. When I'd left, there'd been a certain amount of tension between Winky and Freddy, particularly on Winky's part. I just hoped the two of them hadn't come to blows and wrecked my office while I'd been out.

When I got there, I couldn't see either of them. If Winky had chased Freddy outside and something had happened to the ferret, I'd never forgive myself.

But then I heard laughter coming from behind the screen: Freddy and Winky were playing cards.

"Hello, you two."

"Do you want me to deal you in?" Winky offered.

"No thanks. I've got a lot of work to do. You two seem to be getting on much better."

"Yeah, you should've told me that Freddy fancies himself as a bit of a card sharp."

"What do you mean, *fancies himself*?" Freddy laughed. "I

could beat you with my eyes closed, brother."

"Dream on."

The two of them were clearly having a great time. I'd obviously been worrying over nothing. Who knew a cat and a ferret could be such good friends?

A little while later, I had a visit from Rebecca, and I could tell as soon as she walked through the door that all was not well.

"Whatever's wrong? Isn't it the full moon tonight? Should you still be here in Washbridge?"

"It's okay as long as I leave before the moon rises. That's not why I'm here, though."

"What is it, Rebecca? Sit down, catch your breath, and then tell me all about it."

"I could be wrong about this, but I think there's trouble brewing. Do you remember I told you about my new neighbours who had been causing a few problems?"

"Yeah. What have they done now?"

"Last night when I came home from work, I was walking up the stairs, and they were a flight above me. They had no idea I was there, and that I could hear every word they said. They were laughing and joking. At first, I thought it was just the usual stupid male banter, but then one of them mentioned that it would be a full moon tonight. The other one said that would give them a clear run at the humans, and that he couldn't wait to tear a few of them apart. It made me sick to my stomach, Jill."

"Could they just have been joking around?"

"It's possible, I guess, but it honestly didn't sound like it. I wasn't sure what to do. If it does turn out to be a joke, I'm going to look really stupid."

"You did the right thing by coming to talk to me. Do you remember when you came to see me before, I told you that I occasionally work with the rogue retrievers?"

"Yes. That's why I came to see you."

"I was talking to Daze and Blaze recently. They told me that a couple of werewolves had been released from prison. Apparently, they should have been tagged to prevent them coming back to the human world, but there was a mix up, and it didn't happen. Daze and Blaze have been trying to track them down."

"Do you think they could be my new neighbours?"

"I've no idea, but if there's even a chance that it's them, it needs investigating. I'll let Daze know just in case."

"You won't say that you got this information from me, will you? I don't want to get in trouble."

"Of course not. I won't mention your name, I promise. If it does turn out that they were just joking, and they're not the ex-cons, then no one need ever know this conversation took place."

"Thanks very much, Jill."

"No problem. Will you and Luther still be able to make dinner next week?"

"Definitely. I'm looking forward to it."

As soon as Rebecca had left, I gave Daze a call.

"Hey, Jill. What's up?"

"I may or may not have some information for you. You know those two werewolves you mentioned the other day; the ones who had been released from prison?"

"What about them?"

"Have you caught them yet?"

"No, they're still on the loose. Why? Do you know

something about them?"

"Possibly. I'm not sure. A friend of mine just came to see me. She lives in that apartment block near the cinema. Do you know the one?"

"Yeah, I know where you mean."

"Apparently, some new neighbours moved in a few days ago, and they've been rather disruptive. Last night, she overheard them talking about today's full moon. They said they were looking forward to tearing a few humans apart."

"Who was it who told you this, Jill?"

"Sorry, Daze, but I promised I wouldn't reveal her name. She's new to the human world, and she's terrified, but I trust her. It's entirely possible that she misunderstood, and that it's just a joke, but I thought you might want to check it out."

"I definitely do. It's not like we have any other leads. Blaze and I will get over there as soon as we can."

"Will you let me know how you get on?"

"Of course I will. Thanks for the tip-off, Jill."

I'd no sooner finished on the call to Daze than my phone rang again. This time it was my darling husband.

"Do you have some news for me on the hotel case, Jack?"

"Yeah. It's good news and bad news, I'm afraid."

"Give me the good news."

"We now know who the mysterious bank account belongs to; the one where the quarter of a million pound payments were sent. It's a company called Restart. Apparently, they specialise in helping people to disappear."

"*Disappear*? What does that mean, exactly?"

"They give them a new identity and relocate them. It's not cheap, though. It comes with a hefty price tag. A quarter of a million pounds to be precise."

"What's the bad news?"

"I'm afraid your client isn't one of Restart's customers."

"How can you be so sure?"

"Our people have been through their books with a fine-tooth comb, and they can account for every one of the quarter of a million pound transfers. None of them came from your guy."

"That's a bit of a blow. What's going to happen to the Restart people?"

"Nothing, probably. We may not like what they do, but it's not actually illegal. It's not like they've relocated anyone who's on the run from the law. From what I can make out, most of the people who have availed themselves of the service did so to avoid expensive divorces. I'm sorry I don't have better news for you."

"That's okay. I'll see you tonight."

That bombshell meant I was now well and truly back to square one. I'd been hoping Jack would confirm that Eddie Broom was one of Restart's clients. But then, according to both Lorraine and Sandra, Eddie didn't have that kind of money, so it shouldn't have come as too much of a surprise.

Behind the screen, Winky and Freddy were still playing cards.

"Are you sure you don't want me to deal you in, Jill?" Winky shouted. "It sounds like you could do with cheering up."

"No thanks. I've got a ton of work to do."

I had no choice but to go right back to the beginning, and reread all my notes again, in the hope that I'd spot something I'd missed the first time.

Two hours later, I was still doing just that.

Everything seemed to hinge on the last time that Eddie Broom had been seen. That was when Sylvia Long had stormed out on him, after an argument. They'd gone out for a meal in a bar near to the hotel. What was the bar called? I quickly located her interview and confirmed it was the Lakeside Tavern. They'd gone there because the menu at the budget hotel wasn't up to much. Why did that name ring a bell? Where had I heard it before?

Then I remembered.

It was in the headline I'd seen when I'd first looked for articles on Eddie's disappearance. I went online and brought up the newspaper article in question. It was from the day after Eddie had vanished, and was about some kind of disruption that had taken place at the Lakeside Tavern. Could that be a coincidence? Had something happened to Eddie after Sylvia had left? There was only one way to find out, so I magicked myself over there.

***

"Hello, love." The man behind the bar had a ginger beard to match his wild, curly hair. "You've timed it just right. Happy hour has just started."

"Isn't three o'clock a little early for happy hour?"

"Not really. It goes on until six."

"Doesn't that make it happy *three hours*?"

"I suppose so, but that doesn't really have the same ring

to it. Can I get you a drink?"

"No, thanks. I was hoping to talk to the manager."

"You're in luck, then because that's me. I shouldn't really be out front, but my waste of space barman hasn't turned up yet. When he does get here, he'll get my boot up his backside. Are you sure you don't want a drink? You look like you could do with one."

"No, I'm good, thanks."

"I'm Graham. How can I help you?"

"Jill. I realise that this is something of a long shot, but I wondered if you might remember a disturbance that took place here about two years ago. It must have been quite a big deal at the time because it ended up on the front page of The Bugle."

"Remember it? I'm hardly likely to forget it. It was an absolute nightmare. The publicity did us no good at all. Takings were down for the next two months, so yes, you could say that I remember it. What's your interest in it?"

"I'm a private investigator. I'm working on a missing person case, and as far as I can make out, the man who went missing was last seen here on the night of the disturbance. He'd come here with his lady friend for a meal, but they had some kind of falling out, and she left early. That was the last anyone saw of him. What can you tell me about the disturbance that took place that night?"

"The strange thing is that it was all caused by just one man. Needless to say, he was drunk. He started by hurling abuse at the staff, then he began to pick fights with the other guests. It all escalated from there. We do get the occasional disturbance in here; it kind of goes with the territory. Normally, it peters out, or my security men put a stop to it. This was different, though. The man was like someone possessed."

"Can you describe him to me?"

"I can do better than that. I still have the CCTV footage."

"Do you normally keep it for so long?"

"No, but we had to make several copies for the police. Would you like to see it?"

"Yes, please."

"You'll have to wait until someone can take over—oh, hang on—here he comes now."

I glanced over at the door where a young man wearing jeans and a denim shirt had just walked in. He looked hungover.

"Good of you to show up, Jimmy."

"Sorry, boss. The bus was late."

"Of course it was. Get yourself behind this bar. This lady and I have some business in the back. Come with me, Jill."

He led the way into a small office. "Grab a seat. I'll bring up the recording for you."

A couple of minutes later, I was watching the footage from that night.

"See that?" Graham pointed. "That's the guy. Watch him."

Just as Graham had described, it had all started slowly. The man was clearly drunk, and he was picking an argument with anyone who came near him. He started pushing people around, and soon a fight broke out. Before long, tables and chairs were flying all over the place.

"Did you see that, Jill? I don't know how he did it. Every time they got close to him, he sent my security guys flying across the room. I've never seen strength like it."

"I see what you mean."

"Is that your guy?"

"No, that's not him, I'm afraid."

"Oh, well. Worth a try, I guess." He stopped the footage.

"I'm sorry to have taken up your time, Graham."

"Don't worry about it. I hope you find him."

"Just out of interest, what happened to the guy who caused all the trouble?"

"The police turned up: a man and a woman. They managed to subdue him and took him away."

"Were they in uniform?"

"Err, no, I don't think they were."

"How did you know they were the police?"

"They said they were. Who else would they have been?"

"Right. Is that on CCTV too?"

"No. That was really weird. The camera stopped working just before they arrived."

"How did they manage to overpower him when your security men couldn't?"

"I don't know. I thought he'd make mincemeat of them, but they had him restrained in no time at all. It was quite impressive."

Now, at least, I knew what had happened to Eddie Broom. He *was* the man on the CCTV footage, but I couldn't tell Graham that. What I'd just been watching was not a man possessed, but a man using the 'power' spell.

Eddie Broom was a wizard. And what's more, I had a good idea who the 'police' who took him away really were.

I made a quick call to Loraine Cross.

"It's Jill. I just have a quick question. Was Eddie adopted by any chance?"

"Yes, he was. Why? Is it relevant?"

"Probably not."

"Why do you—"

"Sorry, Lorraine, I have a call on the other line. I'll get back to you as soon as I know anything."

Bingo!

Chapter 24

I was just about to give Daze a call when she phoned me.

"Jill, I wanted to let you know that your friend's neighbours turned out to be the guys we've been looking for."

"Really? That's brilliant."

"It's a good job we acted when we did because it's quite obvious that they'd intended to cause mayhem tonight; there would have been a bloodbath. I know your friend doesn't want you to give out her name, but please tell her from me that she did the right thing, and I'd really like to thank her in person. Of course, I'll understand if she'd rather not."

"Where are her neighbours now?"

"Where they should be: Behind bars. And, this time, they'll be there for a very long time. If or when they ever get out, I will personally supervise their tagging to ensure there's no repeat of this debacle. Anyway, thanks again for the tip-off, Jill."

"Before you go, Daze, I was just about to call you. I wonder if I might ask a favour?"

"After what you've just done? Absolutely. Ask away. What can I do for you?"

"This relates to something that dates back a couple of years. There was a disturbance in a bar called The Lakeside Tavern here in Washbridge. I've just been watching footage of it and—"

"Let me stop you there, Jill. I remember that particular case. Blaze and I were called out to a wizard who'd gone crazy. From what I remember, he was smashed out of his head, and he was using magic to throw things around, and to resist the security men. Is that the guy you're talking about?"

"Yeah, that's him. His name is Eddie Broom."

"What's your interest in him?"

"I was recently hired by his sister to try and find him. He's been missing for two years and the police have pretty much given up on the case. I'd more or less reached a dead end, but then I made a breakthrough. The last place that Eddie was seen was at the Lakeside Tavern; he and his lady friend had dinner there. Then, I remembered a headline I'd seen in The Bugle when I'd been looking at newspapers published around the date of the disappearance. There had been a serious disturbance there on the night that Eddie went missing. On the strength of that, I went to see the manager of the Lakeside Tavern who still had the CCTV footage from that night. As soon as I saw it, I realised that Eddie was a wizard. The manager said the police had taken Eddie away, but my guess is, that it was you guys."

"You're right. It was Blaze and me. I remember it well."

"You wouldn't happen to know where Eddie is now, would you?"

"I know exactly where he is. He's behind bars in Candlefield."

"I should have realised. How long does he have left to serve?"

"I'm not sure. Another year or two, I'd guess."

"Is there any chance that I could talk to him?"

"Normally, I'd say no, but give me a few minutes, and I'll make a couple of phone calls."

"Okay, thanks."

"I'll get back to you as soon as I know one way or the other."

***

While I was waiting to hear back from Daze, I decided to pop into Kathy's shop.

"Whoa, what's going on with you, Jill?" Kathy said. "I don't see you in here for weeks on end and then you come in twice in as many days."

"I was just passing."

"Would you like a drink?"

"Not for me, thanks."

"Are you sure you're all right? That's twice now you've refused a drink."

"I'm fine. I'm busy, that's all. I just wanted to check if Lizzie was okay."

"Why do you keep asking about Lizzie? I told you, she's absolutely fine."

"She's not been acting weird again, then?"

"No. That was something and nothing anyway. I've moved past that. I don't know why you haven't."

"What about Mikey? Is he still having those nightmares about Lizzie?"

"No, he's fine too. Honestly, they're both okay. There's really nothing for you to worry about."

"You're right. I'm just being an over-anxious auntie. Anyway, I'd better get going."

"Are you sure you're okay, Jill? You're the only one who's been acting weird recently."

"Of course I am. I'll catch you later."

Although I was pleased that Lizzie was back to her old self, I had no idea if Martin had played any part in her recovery or not. I gave him another call, not really expecting him to pick up.

He did; on the first ring. "Hi, Jill."

"Martin. I've been trying to get hold of you for ages."

"Sorry, I've been really busy."

"What happened with this red grave thing?"

"Lizzie should be okay now. She is, isn't she?"

"Yeah, Kathy says she's back to her old self."

"That's good. I thought she would be."

"Yes, but what exactly did you do?"

"It's complicated."

"Then we should get together so you can explain it to me."

"You're right. We should, but, honestly, I can't do it just now, I'm extremely busy. Sorry, but I really do have to go."

"Hold on—" It was too late. He'd already hung up. I called him straight back but there was no reply. What was it with this man? First, I couldn't get rid of him, and now, he didn't have time for me. And what was all that red grave mumbo jumbo? Was he really in the 'other' Candlefield? Was there even such a place? All of this was doing my head in.

On my way back up the high street, I bumped into Norman.

"Hi, young man, how goes it?"

"Hello, Jill. I'm okay, thanks."

"How was Hawaii? You've come back with a good tan."

"It was really hot. I had to wear a hat and flip-flops."

"How about Tonya? Did she enjoy herself?"

"Yeah, she did."

"Is she back at the shop?"

"No, she's still in Hawaii."

"How come?"

"While we were there, we decided we'd try our hand at surfing, so we booked a course of lessons. I wasn't very good at it; I kept falling off the board, so I didn't bother again after the first day. Tonya really enjoyed it, though, so she kept up the lessons all week."

"I still don't understand why she's back in Hawaii. Did she fall off the board and hurt herself or something?"

"No, nothing like that. She became rather friendly with the surfing instructor. In fact, they had a bit of a fling. His name is Corey. He has blonde hair and abs. On our last day there, she told me that she didn't love me anymore, and that she was going to stay in Hawaii with Corey."

"I'm really sorry to hear that, Norman."

"That's okay. I still have my bottle tops."

Poor guy.

***

I was just about to go into the office building when my phone rang.

"Wow, Daze, that was quick."

"These things don't take long when you know who to speak to. I've had a word with the powers-that-be and it's okay for you to talk to Edward Broom."

"That's great. How quickly can it be arranged?"

"You can see him right now if you pop over straight away."

"Really?"

"Yeah, I'll meet you outside the gates at Candlefield Prison."

"Okay, I'm on my way."

I was gobsmacked to find Daze wearing a dress.

"Well, look at you." I grinned.

"Don't you start. I've had enough of Blaze taking the mickey."

"Where are you off to dressed like that?"

"If you must know, I have a date."

"Who with?"

"None of your business. Do you want to talk to this guy or not?"

"Sorry, yeah."

"Come on, then." She flashed her ID at the guard, which got us through the gates in double-quick time.

"Are you coming in with me?" I asked.

"No. I'm just going to make sure you get in without any problems, then I'll shoot off."

In the main reception, Daze spoke to the guard behind the desk, who then made a quick phone call. "That's all been cleared. Mrs Maxwell can go through and see Mr Broom, but only for fifteen minutes."

"That's fine," I said. "That'll be more than enough time."

"Okay, Jill," Daze started for the exit. "I'm going to leave you to it."

"Enjoy your date. And I expect all the gory details."

"No chance."

Compared to the CCTV footage I'd watched, Edward Broom seemed to have aged ten years. And, if I wasn't mistaken, he'd lost quite a bit of weight too.

"Hello, Mr Broom. Is it all right if I call you Eddie?"

"Sure. I don't have any idea what this is all about. Someone came to see me a few minutes ago and said I had a visitor. I never get visitors."

"My name is Jill Maxwell."

"Should I know you?"

"No. I work in the human world as a private investigator. I was hired by your sister to try and trace you."

He suddenly became much more animated. "Lorraine's been looking for me?"

"What did you expect? She's been worried sick ever since you vanished."

"Poor Lorraine. I never intended to hurt her. I'm such an idiot. What about Sandra? Is she looking for me too?"

"Your wife? I don't think so."

"Why aren't I surprised? Still, good riddance. I don't know why I ever married that woman. Has anyone else been after me?"

"If by *anyone else* you mean Sylvia Long, then yes, she has."

"You know about Sylvia?"

"Yes, I do. I've spoken to her."

"Our marriage was more or less over. Sylvia made me happy."

"Not happy enough to leave Sandra, apparently."

"I was an idiot. I should have left her long before then. That's what caused the argument that night. Sylvia was fed up of waiting for me to leave Sandra."

"She told me all about it. I've also seen the CCTV footage from the night in question."

"I'm so ashamed of what I did. I was drunk, and I lost my head, but I should never have used magic. I deserve to be in here."

"How much longer do you have to serve?"

"Provided that I behave myself, I have another year inside. Then a further year before I'm allowed to go back to the human world. What will you tell Lorraine?"

"I'm not sure. I can hardly say you're in prison in the paranormal world, can I?"

"I guess not."

"Look, I've had an idea. Let me run it by you and see what you think."

***

After I'd left Candlefield Prison, I magicked myself back to the office where I expected to find Winky and Freddy still playing cards, but Winky was on the sofa glaring at Freddy, who was sitting on my desk.

You could have cut the atmosphere with a knife.

"What's wrong with you two?"

"It's him," Winky pointed. "He's a card cheat."

"I did not cheat," Freddy said. "I don't need to cheat to beat you."

"He's taken all of my money, and I want it back."

"I won that money fair and square, but you'll get a chance to win it back the next time I come here."

"What do you mean, *next time*?" Winky scowled. "I don't ever want to see you back here again."

"It's too late for that, Winky," I said. "I've already told Freddy that he can come in every now and then." I checked my watch. "It's time you and I were going,

Freddy. You'd better get back in my bag."

"Do I have to go in there again? It's dark and it smells."

"If you want to come here occasionally, you're going to have to put up with being in the bag for a few minutes. Now, are you going to get in or do I have to put you in there?"

Reluctantly, he climbed inside. "See you, Winky."

"See you, cheat."

"I'm going to call it a day, Mrs V."

"Okay, dear. Have a nice weekend."

"You too."

Just then she glanced down at my bag. "What have you got in there?"

"Sorry?"

"I saw something move in your bag."

"You must be mistaken. I'd better get going, bye."

When I got out onto the landing, I collared Freddy. "I told you to keep still."

"That's easier said than done. The lining makes me itch."

"Tough. If you don't keep still, I won't bring you here again."

***

Back home, I went straight across the road and knocked on the Normals' door. Norm answered, looking particularly sorry for himself.

"Hello, Jill. What can I do for you?"

"Actually, Norman, it's more a question of what I can do for *you*." I reached into my bag and pulled out the ferret.

"Freddy!" Norm's face lit up, and he shouted, "Naomi, come and see. Jill has found our little boy."

Naomi came running to the door and snatched Freddy out of my hands. "Where did you find this little fellow?"

"He was in our back garden. He seems to be okay."

"He does, doesn't he? Thank you so much, Jill. Freddy, you're a naughty boy. You had Mummy and Daddy really worried. Where have you been all day?"

"Thanks again, Jill," Norm said.

"Don't mention it. Consider it my good deed of the day."

***

"I'm sorry I didn't have better news for you regarding the Restart case," Jack said.

"Don't worry about it. I've solved the case anyway."

"How come? I thought that had set you back to square one."

"It did, but when I went through my notes again, I spotted a connection between the last place Sylvia Long had seen Eddie, and an article I'd read in The Bugle about a disturbance that took place on the same night at the Lakeside Tavern. Luckily for me, the restaurant still had the CCTV footage from that night. It was Eddie; he was drunk, throwing things around and fighting. And it was obvious to me that he was using magic."

"So, he's a wizard?"

"That's right. He was adopted by human parents."

"I thought you were the only one that had happened to."

"Apparently not. The rogue retrievers arrived at the Lakeside Tavern and took him away."

"Where is he now?"

"Serving time in Candlefield Prison. I went to see him this afternoon."

"How did you wangle that?"

"I have friends in high places. He's full of remorse for what he did."

"How much longer will he be in there?"

"He has another year to serve, and then it'll be a further year before he can return to the human world."

"What have you told your client?"

"Nothing yet. I figured I'd take tonight to work out exactly what I'm going to say. Obviously, I can't tell her the truth."

"Rather you than me."

"By the way, I saw Yvonne today."

"How is she? Are she and dad still arguing?"

"It sounds like they've both realised how stupid they were being, and they've managed to reach some kind of compromise."

"Thank goodness for that."

"I also found the Normals' ferret."

"I didn't know they had one."

"He's called Freddy. He sneaked into my car and spent the day at work with me."

"What did Winky make of that?"

"He wasn't very happy at first, but then they got playing cards, and everything seemed to be okay. Until Freddy won, that is."

Chapter 25

"Some Saturday this turned out to be," Jack moaned.

We were still at the kitchen table, having just finished breakfast. He and I both had to work today. I was hoping I'd be done by lunchtime because the only thing I needed to do was to go and see Lorraine Cross, but Jack was expecting to be at work all day.

"Yeah, it sucks," I said. "How come we're the only people in all of Washbridge who have to work weekends?"

"I'm pretty sure we're not the only ones. Look, I tell you what, Jill, why don't we go away next weekend?"

"Can we afford to?"

"No, but even we're allowed to indulge ourselves occasionally. Where do you fancy?"

"I don't know."

"We could go to the seaside. Or what about London? We could take in a show."

"Yeah, that sounds great."

"If I get the chance later today, I'll take a look online and see if there are any bargains to be had."

Jack had left for work and I was just about to do the same when I heard a noise coming from the back of the house. I glanced out the front window and noticed that there was a white van parked on the road. On the side of it was printed:

Hart of Glass

I could see our new window cleaner sitting in the driver's seat, so who was that at the back of the house? I went through to the kitchen, and got the shock of my life;

a robot was staring in at me while he cleaned the window.

I grabbed my bag, locked the door on my way out of the house, walked over to the van, and knocked on the side window.

He lowered the window. "You made me jump, love."

"Sorry."

"I hope we didn't wake you up just now."

"No, we've been up for a while. What's that thing cleaning the windows?"

"That's Robbie. Robbie the robot."

"I've never heard of a robot cleaning windows before."

"That's because this is cutting edge stuff. There's only three of them in the country so far, and I've got one of them."

"How does it work, exactly?"

"It's all quite simple." He picked up what looked like a controller for a games console. "I use this to control Robbie."

"Is it safe?"

"Perfectly. It's all been thoroughly tested. You have absolutely nothing to worry about. Your windows will be spotless."

"Okay, well, I'd better get going. I'll leave you and Robbie to it."

I was just about to get into the car when Norm Normal came running across the road.

"Hold on, Jill!"

"I was just on my way to work."

"I won't keep you for more than a minute. I just wanted to give you this." He handed me a soft toy: a ferret. "It's just our way of saying thank you for returning Freddy to us."

"Err, thanks, but you really shouldn't have bought me anything."

"We didn't. We have dozens of these in the house."

Of course they did.

"Right. Thanks very much, Norm."

***

When I'd called ahead to tell Lorraine Cross that I was coming over, she'd done her best to try to get me to tell her what I knew over the phone, but I'd insisted that we needed to speak face-to-face.

I didn't even get a chance to knock on the door before she answered it.

"Jill, just tell me, is he dead? Is Eddie dead?"

"No, he's not. He's alive and well."

"Thank goodness." She broke down and began to cry. "I really thought I'd lost him."

I took her by the arm, led her through to the lounge, and helped her onto the sofa. "Sit there for a while and catch your breath."

"I'm okay, honestly. Now that I know he's alive, I'll be fine. Where is he?"

"It's all a bit complicated, I'm afraid."

"I don't care, just as long as he's okay. Please tell me where he is."

"I don't actually know."

"But you just said he was okay. How can you know that if you don't know where he is?"

"I'll try to explain as best I can. In the course of my

investigations, I came across a company called Restart."

"What does that have to do with Eddie?"

"The company specialises in providing people with new identities, and then relocating them. People who want to vanish."

"Are you saying that Eddie used this company's services to help him disappear?"

"That's right. Most of their customers are in the same position as Eddie."

"I don't know what you mean. What *position*?"

"People, mainly men, who are in unhappy marriages, and who want to vanish to avoid messy and costly divorces."

"I knew that he and Sandra had been having problems, but I didn't think he'd resort to something as drastic as this. Why didn't he just get a divorce?"

"I don't know the ins and outs, or why he made the decision that he did. I just know that Eddie availed himself of this company's services."

"How did you manage to get in touch with him?"

"It wasn't easy, but I was able to speak to him on the phone. He couldn't, or wouldn't, tell me where he is, but he did ask me to convey a message to you. He wanted me to tell you that he's happy and well, and that he's very sorry for all the upset he's caused you."

"How could he do something like this? How could he vanish without a word to me? I don't understand. We were so close."

"If it's any consolation, I can tell that he regrets his decision now. In fact, he was close to tears when he was talking to me."

"Is that it, then? Will I never see him again?"

"Don't give up hope yet. There's still a possibility you might see him again."

"How?"

"The last thing I want to do is to get your hopes up, but I got the feeling that Eddie would like to contact you."

"So why doesn't he? What's stopping him? He spoke to you, why can't he speak to me?"

"He said it was something to do with having to fulfil his part of the contract first."

"What contract?"

"The one he made with Restart. Anyone who uses their services has to agree not to return, or make contact with anyone from their past life, within a certain period of time. If they do, it would undermine the company's operations, and would result in a massive fine for the person who reneged on the contract. He seemed to suggest that he might be in a position to make contact with you in two years' time."

"So, I'll be able to see him in two years?"

"Possibly, but don't go pinning all your hopes on that."

"How do I know you're not just making all of this up, Jill? You have to admit that it sounds kind of farfetched."

"It does, I agree, but I promise you, he's alive and well. I anticipated that you might be sceptical, so I asked Eddie to tell me something that only you and he would know. He said to say poor Hicky."

She broke down again.

"Are you okay?"

"I'm fine. Hicky was Eddie's pet mouse. He wasn't supposed to let it out of the cage, but one day when Mum was out, he did, and next-door's cat got it."

"Poor Hicky."

Although Lorraine Cross had been grateful for the work I'd done, she'd been left feeling rather hollow. On the one hand, she now knew that her brother was alive and well. On the other, she was clearly devastated that Eddie had chosen to leave without a word. And, of course, she still didn't know if she'd ever see him again. It wasn't the ideal outcome, but I consoled myself that it was the best I could have hoped for under the circumstances.

When I'd run my plan past Eddie, he hadn't been happy that Lorraine would think he'd deliberately left without a word, but as I pointed out to him, what else could I say? I certainly couldn't tell her the truth: That he was a wizard locked up in a jail in the paranormal world. And, if she decided to double check the Restart angle, she would find that such a company did exist.

**

As Jack was going to be working all day, I thought I might as well pop into town. I would grab lunch, and then have a mosey around the shops for a couple of hours.

After I'd eaten (just a sandwich because I wasn't particularly hungry), I decided to check out some of the side streets, which I rarely visited.

"Jill!" It was Kathy; she was with Peter and the kids.

"Hey there, you four."

"Where's Jack?"

"He had to work. I've been working too, but I've finished now, so I thought I'd do a bit of shopping before I go home. I'll tag along with you guys if you don't mind."

"Sorry, Jill, but we have to leave in a few minutes.

Mikey and Pete are going fishing, and Lizzie's friend and her mum are coming over. You're welcome to join us if you like."

"No, thanks. When I've done here, I'm going to go home and put my feet up."

"Come on, Dad." Mikey pulled at his father's sleeve. "Let's go inside."

"Sorry, Jill," Peter said. "I'll have to take him in here or my life won't be worth living."

They both disappeared into a fishing tackle shop.

"Pete promised to buy him a new rod," Kathy said.

"I didn't realise this shop was here."

"It only opened a couple of weeks ago. Have you seen the name?" She grinned.

"Tommy's Tackle?" I laughed. "Brilliant."

"Would you mind staying with Lizzie for a couple of minutes while I nip to the loo?"

"Sure." Kathy shot off up the street.

"Mummy bought me a unicorn kit, Auntie Jill."

"Wow, that sounds great."

"It is. You have to put it together."

"How have you been, Lizzie? You were a little under the weather the last time I saw you."

"I'm okay, but I've had a few nasty dreams."

"Oh dear. What kind of nasty dreams?"

"I dreamt that some red mist was following me around, and I couldn't get away from it."

"That doesn't sound very nice."

"Mummy said they were only dreams, and I should forget about them."

"That sounds like good advice."

Not long after Kathy had returned, Peter and Mikey

came out of the shop. Mikey was carrying the longest fishing rod I'd ever seen.

"How on earth are we supposed to get that in the car?" Kathy said.

"Don't panic," Peter reassured her. "It comes apart. Mikey just wanted to show it to you."

"Right. Well, it's very nice, but you'd better take it to pieces before it has someone's eye out."

I was troubled by what Lizzie had told me about her dreams. Red mist? Was that in some way connected to red grave? I needed to get to the bottom of this once and for all, and the only way to do that was to speak to Martin, so I gave him a call.

"Martin, it's me. I need to see you right now."

"I'm sorry, Jill, but like I told you yesterday, I'm really busy at the moment."

"I don't care how busy you are. I'm going to my office now, and I expect you to be there within the next fifteen minutes. If you're not, then you and I are done, and I never want to see or hear from you again."

"But, Jill, please let me explain."

"Be there in fifteen minutes or don't bother to contact me ever again."

I ended the call and made my way to my office building.

There were voices coming from behind the screen; Winky and three other cats were playing cards.

"What are you doing here on a Saturday?" he said. "Haven't you got anything better to do?"

"I've been working. How come you're playing cards?

After what happened with Freddy, I didn't—"

"Can I have a word?" He jumped out of his chair, and led me across to the other side of the office. "Keep it down."

"What's wrong?"

"Those guys don't need to know about cheating Freddy."

"I would have thought you'd have learned your lesson after losing all your money to a ferret."

"That's precisely why I'm playing. I need to get my money back somehow. That's why the fish are here."

"You have fish here too? Where are they?"

"Not *fish*, fish." He rolled his eyes. "I've explained all of this before. A fish is what you call someone who thinks they're good at cards, but who always ends up losing."

"Like you, you mean?"

"Shut up. I have to get back to the game."

There were only two minutes to go, and it didn't look like Martin was going to show. That was fine by me. I'd managed without a brother this far, and I could do so again. It would be no great loss.

I was just about to leave when he suddenly appeared in the centre of the room.

"Martin, what on earth happened to you?"

His face was bruised, one of his eyes was swollen shut, and there was a cut on his forehead.

"I apologise for my appearance, Jill." He limped over to my desk and sank down into the chair. "I had a bit of a problem getting to the red graves."

"It looks like it. What kind of problem?"

"They're protected by creatures called snatchers.

They're a bit of a rough bunch."

"And they did this to you?"

"Yeah, but you should see the other guys." He tried to laugh but just winced.

"Why didn't you tell me you were injured?"

"I didn't want to worry you. That's why I said I was busy. I thought if I could buy myself a few days to recover, you need never know."

"That's stupid. I've just seen Lizzie. She said she's been having nightmares about red mist."

"You don't need to worry about that; that's just the aftereffects. It'll soon wear off. She's perfectly safe now."

"I don't know what to make of any of this. How do I know there's such a thing as red graves, or that there's even another Candlefield?"

"Just look at the state of me. I certainly didn't do this to myself."

"Maybe not, but it could have happened anywhere. You could've been hit by a bus for all I know."

"Give me your hand, Jill."

"Why?"

"Just give me your hand."

Chapter 26

That had been one freaky experience. Apart from the occasional trip with Grandma, I was usually the one who magicked people from place to place, so it felt quite weird for Martin to do it.

I looked around, trying to get my bearings. We appeared to be in the middle of a vast area of scrubland.

"Where are we, Martin?"

"Can you see the forest over there in the distance? The red graves are in a clearing through there."

"But where is this place?"

"Candlefield. My Candlefield."

"But this is nothing like the Candlefield I know."

"Yes, it is. There are vast areas just like this outside of the city. You must have travelled over them when you've been to CASS."

"But how do I know we're in *your* Candlefield? This could be *my* Candlefield. It could even be the human world."

"We really don't have time for this discussion right now. Do you want to see the red graves or not?"

"Yes, sorry."

"Okay, follow me. When we get to the forest, you must keep very quiet because the snatchers have exceptional hearing."

He led the way across the scrubland—our pace was quite slow because Martin was still limping.

When we reached the edge of the forest, he stopped, and said in a hushed voice, "It's about another five-minute walk from here. Keep quiet and stay very close to me."

As soon as we were in amongst the trees, hundreds of little flies began to attack my legs, arms and face.

"Ouch."

"Be quiet, Jill. The snatchers will hear you."

"Sorry, but these flies are trying to eat me alive." I swatted another one off my nose.

"Look over there." He pointed. "Can you see it?"

I followed his gaze to the clearing where the ground was covered by row upon row of red rectangles.

"Is this some kind of graveyard?" I whispered.

"They aren't actually graves. That's just what people call it because the red rectangles look like tiny graves. And because of what's under there, obviously."

"What is under there?"

"A facsimile of the person whose energy they are draining."

"*Facsimile*? You mean a copy?"

"Yes. After the snatchers have grabbed their victims and brought them back here, they —"

"Hold on. Are you saying that when Lizzie disappeared that day, she ended up here?"

"That's right."

"But she was gone for less than an hour."

"That's all it takes. The snatcher makes a facsimile of the victim, buries it beneath one of those red rectangles, and then returns the victim. The facsimile slowly drains the energy and life from the remote victim until the poor soul dies."

"That's horrible. How did the snatchers get to the human world?"

"That's puzzling me too. All the victims I've known until now lived here in *my* Candlefield. I have no idea how they managed to get to the human world, but I suspect they may have had help from someone or something."

"How did you stop them draining the life from Lizzie?"

"By destroying her facsimile. It's the only way."

"But there are dozens of them, hundreds probably. How did you know which rectangle contained Lizzie's facsimile?"

"I didn't. I started at one end and worked my way along until I found her."

"That must have taken you ages."

"I got lucky. I found the right rectangle on the second row that I checked. It's not finding the facsimile that's the problem. It's fighting off the snatchers while you're trying to do it."

"Where are the snatchers?"

Just then, a rabbit shot out of the forest and ran across the clearing. Before it had got halfway across, dozens of small, horrible creatures appeared. They had short legs, square bodies, and very long arms with razor-like pincers for hands. To my horror, they tore the poor little bunny apart.

"There's no wonder you were so badly hurt, Martin. I'm sorry I didn't believe you."

"That's okay, but we'd better get going now before the snatchers sense we're here."

"Hold on. Are you telling me that each of those red rectangles contains a facsimile of someone, and that the facsimile is sucking the energy from that poor soul?"

"Most of them will, yes."

"In that case, we can't just leave. We have to do something about it."

"Don't be ridiculous, Jill. The snatchers will destroy us."

"I can't leave, knowing that there are other people suffering like Lizzie did."

Ignoring Martin's protests, I stepped out into the clearing, and began to walk towards the rectangles. I hadn't got very far before the snatchers spotted me and started in my direction.

I shot a thunderbolt at each one in turn, blasting them to smithereens. The problem was that as soon as I destroyed one, another one appeared. There were simply too many of them; it would only be a matter of time before I was overwhelmed.

Suddenly, Martin appeared at my side, which made it a much more even contest. The battle raged hard and long, with both of us sustaining a number of minor injuries, but eventually all of the snatchers had been destroyed.

"That was fun," I said.

"You have a very strange idea of *fun*, Jill."

"How do we destroy the facsimiles?"

"That's the easy part." He walked over to the first red rectangle and blasted it with a thunderbolt, leaving just a smoking hole in the ground.

We worked our way along each row until they'd all been zapped.

"Is that it?" I said. "Are they gone?"

"For now, yes, but they'll be back. They always are."

"Why aren't there any snatchers in *my* Candlefield?"

"I have no idea, but thank your lucky stars that there aren't." He took a deep breath. "I think we deserve a drink and some cake."

"That sounds like a plan."

He took my hand again, and this time we landed in a

busy street.

"Where are we?" I asked.

"Don't you recognise it?"

"Err, I feel like I should."

"Follow me." He led the way down the road, and around the corner, where we came across a shop that looked very familiar indeed.

"That looks like—"

"Cuppy C? Yes, but look at the sign."

"Bunny B?"

"Let's go inside and I'll introduce you to the twins."

***

Rocky and Stone, the twins who ran Bunny B, were an absolute delight, and just like my cousins, they were constantly bickering with one another. I'd asked Martin if he thought I should mention Cuppy C to them. He said it was probably best not to because we were the only ones who knew there were two Candlefields, and it might just confuse them.

"What do you think of this place?" Martin said.

"I like it. The coffee is delicious."

"What about the muffin? You've only eaten half of it."

"It's nice, but I seem to have lost my appetite. I think it must be all the adrenaline from the fighting. I'm not sure about the shop name, though."

"Bunny B? What's wrong with it?"

"Cuppy C works, so does Cakey C, but Bunny B? It makes me think of rabbits and bumblebees. Anyway, Martin, I just wanted to tell you that I'm really sorry that I doubted you, and for all the horrible things I said."

"Don't give it a second thought. It's understandable under the circumstances."

"Even so, I shouldn't have been so dismissive. You are my brother, after all. I should have trusted you."

"You're right." He grinned. "In future, please be sure to listen to your big brother."

I thumped his arm. "I'd better get going. I'll see you again soon."

***

Back in the human world, I checked my phone to see if I'd missed any calls from Jack. I hadn't, but there were a number of texts from Amber, Pearl and Aunt Lucy.

The first one, from Aunt Lucy, said that they'd heard my waxwork was now on display. She, Lester, and the twins were headed over there, and she wanted me to join them.

Oh no! This could not be happening!

The second message was from Amber and simply said, "Where are you, Jill?"

The third message, from Pearl, said, "Hurry up, Jill. You're going to miss the big reveal."

The most recent message, which had arrived just a few minutes earlier, was from Amber. It read simply, "LOL."

I was just about to put my phone away when it beeped with another message. This one was from Pearl, and had a photo attached: It was a photo of my waxwork on display in the Candlefield Wax Museum.

Filled with dread, I magicked myself over there.

A sign at the entrance pointed the way to the gallery's newest exhibits. A large crowd had gathered around them, but I managed to fight my way to the front, only to come face-to-face with my horrific waxwork, which was standing on a plinth with my name on it.

"Jill, come and join us," Aunt Lucy shouted. "What happened to your arms and legs?"

"It's nothing. I fell into a holly bush."

"Your waxwork is very — err — "

"It's awful. It should never have been put out on display. I told them not to do it."

The twins were clearly struggling not to laugh.

"I think it's really good," Amber said.

"Yeah, such a great likeness." Pearl giggled.

"Shut up, you two. It doesn't look anything like me."

Suddenly, Grandma appeared. "You're perfectly right, Jill. It doesn't look anything like you."

"Thank you, Grandma."

"It's much better looking than you."

I couldn't bear to stay there for another minute, so I told Aunt Lucy that I was leaving.

"Before you go, Jill, I just wanted to say thank you for setting Lester up with that job."

"I wasn't sure how you'd feel about it."

"To be honest, I'm not crazy about the smell of fish, but it's better than him having to deal with dead bodies all day. Or slaying dragons."

***

When I arrived home, I was surprised to find Jack's car on the driveway.

"Are you all right, Jill?" he said. "You're covered in cuts and bruises."

"Yeah, I'm fine."

"You don't look fine. Whatever happened to you?"

"I was with Martin. We had a run-in with some snatchers."

"With *what*?"

"They're the things that tried to suck the life out of Lizzie. Anyway, how come you're back already? I thought you had to work all day."

"We got done sooner than I expected. I've only just walked in, actually, and I'm afraid I have some bad news."

"What now?"

"I think we've been burgled."

"What makes you say that? Is something missing?"

"I'm not sure. I haven't had the chance to check yet, but one of the windows in the kitchen is broken."

I walked through and saw the broken glass on the worktop.

"That wasn't burglars."

"How do you know?"

"The window cleaner must have done that. He arrived not long after you left this morning. He was using a robot called Robbie to clean the windows."

"A robot window cleaner? I've never heard of those before."

"Neither had I, but Mr Hart reckoned it was cutting edge stuff. He assured me that it was tried and tested, and that there was nothing to worry about. Did he leave a note to acknowledge the breakage?"

"Not that I've seen."

"In that case, he and I will need to have words."

Just then my phone beeped with another message,

which I assumed would be from the twins, continuing to ridicule my waxwork. It was actually from Kathy; it was a photo of Mikey holding a large fish.

"I bumped into Kathy, Peter and the kids earlier. They were buying a new fishing rod for Mikey, and judging by this photo, it looks like it did the trick."

"Let me see." Jack took the phone from me. "That is a whopper, isn't it?"

"I'll make a cup of tea." I grabbed the kettle.

"Wow!" Jack said. "What's this ugly thing?"

"I don't know, Jack. A carp? A trout, maybe? I'm not very well up on fish."

"I don't mean the fish. I'm talking about this waxwork."
Oh bum!

ALSO BY ADELE ABBOTT

The Witch P.I. Mysteries
(A Candlefield/Washbridge Series)

Witch Is When... (Season #1)
Witch Is When It All Began
Witch Is When Life Got Complicated
Witch Is When Everything Went Crazy
Witch Is When Things Fell Apart
Witch Is When The Bubble Burst
Witch Is When The Penny Dropped
Witch Is When The Floodgates Opened
Witch Is When The Hammer Fell
Witch Is When My Heart Broke
Witch Is When I Said Goodbye
Witch Is When Stuff Got Serious
Witch Is When All Was Revealed

Witch Is Why... (Season #2)
Witch Is Why Time Stood Still
Witch is Why The Laughter Stopped
Witch is Why Another Door Opened
Witch is Why Two Became One
Witch is Why The Moon Disappeared
Witch is Why The Wolf Howled
Witch is Why The Music Stopped
Witch is Why A Pin Dropped
Witch is Why The Owl Returned
Witch is Why The Search Began
Witch is Why Promises Were Broken
Witch is Why It Was Over

Witch Is How... (Season #3)
Witch is How Things Had Changed
Witch is How Berries Tasted Good
Witch is How The Mirror Lied
Witch is How The Tables Turned
Witch is How The Drought Ended
Witch is How The Dice Fell
Witch is How The Biscuits Disappeared
Witch is How Dreams Became Reality
Witch is How Bells Were Saved
Witch is How To Fool Cats
Witch is How To Lose Big
Witch is How Life Changed Forever

Witch Is Where... (Season #4)
Witch is Where Magic Lives Now

Susan Hall Investigates
(A Candlefield/Washbridge Series)
Whoops! Our New Flatmate Is A Human.
Whoops! All The Money Went Missing.
Whoops! Someone Is On Our Case.
Whoops! We're In Big Trouble Now.

Murder On Account (A Kay Royle Novel)

Web site: AdeleAbbott.com
Facebook: facebook.com/AdeleAbbottAuthor

Printed in Great Britain
by Amazon